OTHER ECHOES

OTHER ECHOES

Adèle Geras

1-7914

David Fickling Books

OXFORD · NEW YORK

Published by David Fickling Books
an imprint of Random House Children's Books
a division of Random House, Inc.
New York

Published simultaneously in Canada by Random House of Canada Limited,
Toronto. Published in Great Britain in 2004 by David Fickling Books, an imprint
of Random House Children's Books. Originally published in 1982 by Atheneum.

"Rose Rose I Love You" words by Wilfred Thomas, arranged by Chris Langdon,
© 1951 Chappell Music Ltd, London W6 8BS, reproduced by permission of
International Music Publications Ltd, all rights reserved.
"I'll See You Again" words and music by Noel Coward, © 1929 Chappell Music
Ltd, London, W6 8BS, reproduced by permission of International Music
Publications Ltd, all rights reserved.

www.randomhouse.com/teens

Library of Congress Cataloging-in-Publication Data
Geras, Adèle.
Other echoes / Adèle Geras.
p.   cm.
SUMMARY: Now eighteen years old and living in England, Flora remembers the
experiences she had as a nine-year-old in North Borneo, or Sabah, where she
endured outsider status and where she uncovered the secret story
of an old house.
ISBN 0-385-75054-4 (trade) — ISBN 0-385-75055-2 (lib. bdg.)
[1. Self-confidence—Fiction. 2. Interpersonal relations—Fiction. 3. Secrets—
Fiction. 4. Memory—Fiction. 5. Sabah—Fiction. 6. Malaysia—Fiction.] I. Title.
PZ7.G29354Ot 2005
[Fic]—dc22
2004008713

Printed in the United States of America
April 2005
10 9 8 7 6 5 4 3 2 1

To Norm

* *

'. . . Other echoes
Inhabit the garden.
Shall we follow?'

*From 'Burnt Norton' by T.S. Eliot
(Four Quartets)*

This room is almost completely white. The curtains and the bedspread are blue, the linoleum is brown, but apart from that, everything is white, from Sister's starchy coat (which would probably creak if she ever sat down) to the little button on the bedside lamp. It's not what you might call a riot of colour outside the window, either. Grey-green grass, grey sea, grey-white clouds thick over the whole sky. Grey. November.

Last night I dreamed I was in another room. Shreds of the dream are still with me although I have been awake for some time, and for a while after I woke up, I couldn't remember where I had seen such a room: high and dark, with the sun sloping through the slats of shutters on to a polished floor. Near the ceiling, the fan turns and turns, stirring up the air, heavy with heat, clicking and whirring its black blades. The room is full of echoes (is it empty?), and there are no ornaments and no carpets, only one photograph in a frame standing on a table near an oil lamp, which has a pattern of ivy leaves cut into the cloudy glass. A man's voice is singing, far away, and piano music runs rippling like water over stones. In the few seconds between sleeping and waking, I heard the words of the song, but they are gone now, leaving hazy images, flashes, feelings in my mind of things I cannot completely capture or describe: a sense of spring, and sadness, and unrequited love, dissolving pictures of small flowers growing beside a stream, of a girl with long hair combing it out in the sunlight, and of a mill-wheel turning. A voice in my head spoke suddenly, and so clearly that I began to turn my head to see who was talking. Of course, there was no one in my little white room, but I remembered the voice. I recognized it. It came from the dream, or from somewhere in my memory, or from the memory of the dream. But what words were spoken? The words have faded, but I knew the room then. I remembered it all.

Perpetual rest is exhausting. Sister brings me restful things to do.

'Here's a jigsaw for you, dear,' she said yesterday, and the watch that hangs from a ribbon pinned to her stiff bosom bounced about as she put the box on my table. 'A lovely picture of the countryside. Just the ticket.'

There are over five hundred pieces, and most of them are blue. Those that are not blue are mostly green. How am I supposed even to begin? And is it worth the effort of finding how they all fit together when I don't even like the picture? I hate jigsaws, I've decided. The result is generally hideous, and anyway beyond my control, and how to achieve a result is beyond my intelligence.

It would be pleasant to be going into a decline. A wasting disease would be very romantic, but alas, I am only tired. They call it nervous exhaustion. The entrance exams for university have taken it out of me. (Taken what?) I should probably still be in school with the others, killing time till the end of term, the end of my schooldays, quite possible the end of my child-hood, had I not fainted (dramatically, and, I like to think, elegantly) in the middle of Mozart's 'Ave Verum' in chapel on Sunday.

So now I am resting in the Sanatorium. The San, which is what everyone else calls it, evokes Malory Towers and other fictional boarding-schools, so I prefer to give it its full title, and imagine that it is an establishment for tubercular poets set high in the Swiss Alps. It is a square, grey building, like a young child's pencil drawing of a house: triangle of roof, square windows set one above the other, rectangular door in the centre. The Sanatorium is five minutes walk from the Main School, along the gravel path, past the Nissen huts and the hockey pitches, past the tennis courts and the gardening sheds, the last outpost of the school empire.

* * *

11

The Head brought some embroidery silks and a tray cloth patterned with flowers. A present from my friends. She doesn't look like a Head. Her fingernails are red, her suits tweedy but stylish, and her hair is short and of that particular shade of grey that says to the observer 'I am chic' rather than 'I am old'. Where are the hearty, frumpish, bunned and gowned school-marms of my Enid Blyton days?

The Head said: 'Embroidery is very relaxing I believe.'

I said: 'Thank you very much.'

Thank you, indeed! Maybe it was Kaye's idea of a joke. Maybe Miss Travis had suggested it and they didn't dare tell her. Maybe they really don't know how hopeless I am with such things. Maybe no one but me has any idea of how grubby, tangled and generally disgusting that tray cloth will look the minute I slip the shiny black paper bracelet off the first tidy little skein, thread my needle and make the first, tentative stab into the linen. And I probably will start on it. I always start, because before the beginning, an Ideal Tray Cloth hovers in my imagination: pearly satin stitch, perfect cross-stitches like rows and rows of tiny stars, all in shimmering rainbow colours, and the back almost indistinguishable from the front – my own work. After a few hours I will remember I cannot embroider. The tray cloth will end up thrust into the depths of my workbag, to lie forever in the company of half-done bits of tapestry and a sad little piece of something or other that I was once sure I was going to knit. Still, unlike the jigsaw, you never know. Perhaps this tray cloth will be the one, the one that comes out right in the end. You never know.

When Miss O'Neill came to see me, I asked her for paper. Lots of it. She returned the same afternoon with three fat exercise books.

'I've brought you these,' she said, smiling. 'I hope they'll do. Whatever are they for? I'm sure you're not supposed to be writing, taxing your brain. What will Sister say?'

'I won't be doing any work, I promise. Just writing.'

'A story? Poems?'

I thought about this.

'Memoirs,' I said.

Miss O'Neill laughed.

'At your age?'

'Memories, then.'

'That's something else again, memories. Memories of anything in particular?'

'No,' I said, 'nothing in particular. I shall just start, and see what happens.'

I was lying of course. Blank pages give you the illusion that they are empty, that anything can happen, any wonder, fable, adventure, romance that you care to invent can be put down; but it is not so. There is always something there, waiting to be written, and ever since the dream, the dream about the room, I have known what it is I want to say.

* * *

Chris, or Vinnie or Steve, would tell a different story, perhaps, but this one is mine, and I shall tell it as truthfully as I can. I have been thinking about it. I remember many things. Sometimes, I can see whole scenes in my head, unrolling like sequences from a film; but eight years have passed since those days, and maybe it was not all as I remember.

When I think of the story I am about to tell, it seems that the bits and pieces floating about in my mind resemble the interlocking chips of wood in Sister's jigsaw. Some are easily fitted together, others I will have to move around to see where they fit in, and still others are lying face down, so that I cannot see what is on them, nor where they might be placed. Perhaps I will turn them over as I write, and then they, too, will have to be found a place in the pattern. But the whole, the pattern, the beginning, middle and end, are all there. It's not like making a patchwork, where you are free to select this design, this fabric, this contrast. Nor is it like a mosaic, where you can choose the colours and the order of the colours and make decisions about what the picture will be like. I have to find the pieces and move them around until they fit. The picture is already there.

I have hardly thought about Borneo at all for years. I have a few ornaments that have survived the twice-yearly burial in a roll of regulation school socks in the top of my trunk: a little turquoise-blue china horse rearing up, almost airborne; a statuette of an old fisherman holding a yellow fish; and a small sandalwood box with a curly, spiralling dragon carved on the lid. I don't notice these things on my chest-of-drawers any more. I never even look at them. They're there, that's all. I will look at them again when I leave here.

1

The first time I saw Jesselton, I was standing on the deck of a small cargo ship. My mother and I had come from Singapore. The ship smelled of copra, a sour, rancid, horrible smell. Every night, my mother went cockroach-hunting in our cabin with a rolled-up air-mail copy of *The Times*, specially kept for the purpose. The white buildings of the town, the red, sloping roofs, the jungle-covered hills and the mauve shadow of the mountain, Kinabalu, beyond them looked like a painting: composed, coloured, textured, not quite real. As the ship approached the dock, I could see flowers climbing up the sides of the houses on the hill.

'Bougainvillaea,' my mother told me. Were there really so many shades of red?

From the car window, driving through the town, I looked at all the other dusty cars and the crowded pavements: women holding live chickens by their feet in a bunch, like squawking flowers; men in shop door-ways playing games, moving small pieces across a wooden board; people running barefoot, talking, waving their arms; and an English family out shopping, the mother in a flower-printed cotton dress and a sun hat, the father in long khaki shorts, like my own father. The girl wore sandals with no socks. She looked much younger than me.

There was a huge crowd on one corner, standing in a ring, shouting. Shouting, and beating their fists in the air. From the centre of the ring rose clouds of dust and feathers.

'What are they doing, Daddy?' I asked.

'Watching a cock fight.'

'Can we have a look?'

'Certainly not.' My mother shivered. 'Drive on, quickly. Horrible, cruel thing! How can they allow it?'

'What do they do?' I wanted to know.

My father said: 'The cocks fight one another, and the one left alive is the winner.'

As we drove past, I could smell blood, like at the butcher's, all mixed up with the dust and the heat.

We drove along a road that followed the line of the coast. At sea level, all the houses were up on stilts.

'Why are the houses on legs?' I asked.

'Wait till you see the rain,' said my father. 'It comes down every day for months, whole Niagaras of it. This road will be a river then, and all the dry grass over there will look more like a rice field.'

Kampong Aya, Village on the Water. A few

palm-thatched huts on shaky-looking stilts leaning against one another in a vast pond of brackish mud. The sea breeze blew the smell of dried fish and over-ripe fruit right into the car.

'Damn,' said Dad as we drove past. 'I forgot to point out the school.'

'Where was it?'

'Opposite Kampong Aya.'

'I didn't notice.'

'You'll see it properly on Monday, and we'll drive past again tomorrow on the way to the Club.'

'Look at the hats!' I shouted. 'Where are they all going?' We had just passed a line of women walking at the side of the road. They had long poles, with a basket hanging at each end, balanced across their shoulders. I wondered how they could walk upright under such weight. Their faces were shaded from the sun by huge conical hats of woven straw, and their wide, black cotton trousers flap-flapped round their ankles as they walked.

Dad said: 'They're going to the market.'

Our house looked like the others we had passed at intervals along the road. Up on smart, white-painted stilts, long and white with a red roof, and a verandah all along one side with steps leading down into the garden.

'Some people have gardens,' said Dad. 'Ours is called a compound.'

'Why?'

'A garden implies some kind of work, and I'm afraid I haven't done any.'

At first I sat on the verandah and wouldn't go in. Yards and yards of polished wooden floor, a few rattan chairs and tables, and hanging from the roof, six halves of coconut husk in which orchids had been planted, not by my father. They frothed over the sides of their brown baskets, spilling and curling down, dangling in the hot breeze that blew off the sea: ice-cream colours, pink and pale green and beige, freckled and stripey, not like proper flowers at all, but like animals, like little dragons.

The house had four rooms running into one another, with a bathroom at each end. Bathroom – little bedroom – dining room – lounge – big bedroom – bathroom. The dining room and the lounge were really one long room. You could tell which bit was which by the furniture. All the armchairs were made of bamboo and had plump cream cushions trimmed with brown piping. The kitchen and pantry were behind the dining room. My bedroom was small. The walls were painted pale blue, and the mosquito net was folded into a gauzy white cloud over the bed. At night, it would be unfolded and hang in the darkness like a white tent from wires strung between the walls, and at bedtime, I would creep into it, making sure to tuck it in again carefully, so that no insects, so that nothing, could get in.

* * *

'Flora, this is your amah, and this is Cook.' My mother and I shook their hands solemnly. I think we were both embarrassed. No one had ever helped Mum in the house before, and I had never had a nanny, or a governess, and didn't know whether to feel proud or resentful. Later, when I learned that every English household with children had an amah, I grew used to it. Now, I realize that we were all pampered and spoilt. Even our beds were made for us, and we thought nothing of it.

Amah was tall and wore a flower-patterned sarong wound round her waist and reaching to her bare feet. Her blouse was white. I suppose she was elderly, but it was hard to tell. Her face was almost perfectly round and smooth, her hair was black and shiny and done up into a knot at the nape of her neck, and she walked upright, padding with soft footsteps like a dancer on her small golden feet.

Cook was younger than Amah, somewhat older than my father. He wore khaki shorts and a khaki shirt and no shoes. His smile was so wide and white that it took up about half his face.

We called them Amah and Cook. I was nearly ten, and I called two adults older even than my parents by the names that went with the work they did. I am ashamed now. I want to call to them, wherever they are, and shout out: 'I'm sorry. I meant no disrespect.' It's only now that I realize that not calling people by their proper names is the beginning, and by the end one group of people can say of another: you are not like us, you are inferior to us, you are not human beings at all. I could say that I did it because the grown-ups did, I was only a child, I didn't understand then. It was customary, that was all. But the grown-ups should have known, they should have learned, shouldn't they?

What could Amah and Cook have thought of me? I was small for my age, and thin, with long, nothing-coloured plaits, and I wore glasses. My dress had puffed sleeves and a gathered skirt and smocking on the bodice. Blue smocking on pink cotton, blue-framed glasses on a pink face. Matching, you might say.

'Who lives over there?' I asked, pointing across the road to a house exactly like our own. We were sitting on the verandah. I was drinking lime juice and rattling the ice-cubes with a spoon. My parents' drinks were the same colour as mine, but they had gin added to theirs.

'The Jameses,' said my father. 'She gives a dancing class we thought you might like to go to. They're very nice.'

'Have they got any children?'

'There's a daughter, I think, At school in England, but no children your age. Would you like to go to the dancing class?'

'Yes, please.'

'I'll talk to Lily James about it, then.'

I looked across at the Jameses' house and thought about dancing again. When I was six, I had wanted to be a ballerina. I knew now that I wasn't good enough, but I loved dancing because while the music was playing, I could forget who I was and turn into someone else: someone bright and beautiful and floating; unconnected with my everyday self.

'I can hear the sea,' I said. 'Is it far away?'

'Far away?' Dad laughed. 'It's just behind those trees. Finish your drink and come and see.'

'She's tired, dear,' said Mum. 'Won't tomorrow do?'

Dad said: 'It's not far, really. Two hundred yards at the most. Why don't you come, too?'

'No, you go, and I'll unpack. It'll wait for me until tomorrow.'

'Right, Flora. Take your socks off, but keep your sandals on till we get to the beach. Don't want you stepping on any snakes.'

'Snakes? Really?'

'Yes, really, and every other kind of creepy-crawly you can think of. But we won't leave the path, and we'll be careful, I promise. You'll have to get used to it.'

'Are they poisonous, Dad?'

'Some are and some aren't, I daresay, but you shouldn't stop to enquire. Avoid the nasty brutes, and if you see one, run like hell.'

'Will we meet one tonight?'

'No, I'm sure we won't. Don't worry. I'll take my

stick, if it'll make you feel better, and any foolhardy snake who cares to tangle with me better beware.'

'Bwana Baxter,' I said laughing. 'Only it's "Tuan" here isn't it, not "Bwana".'

'Me, Tarzan,' said Dad, taking my hand. 'You Jane.'

Green. Green everywhere. Thick, moist, dark. Palm trees, fronds, vines, ferns uncurling in the small spots of sunlight filtering through the overhanging leaves. At the end of the green tunnel, sand like talcum powder blew under my feet. There was the sea, royal blue, turquoise, aquamarine, clear emerald, cloudy jade: all the blues and greens in the world lying in swirls and stripes from the shore to the horizon. Waves spread themselves out, one after another, on the sand, like pretty skirts frilled with white crochet.

We found a jellyfish washed up on the damp shore, a horrible pinkish and blueish and greyish creature, like left-over jelly at a party, all blobby and soft. I poked about in it with a stick. Afterwards, I felt sorry that I had. Poor jellyfish. I wouldn't like to have all my squashy bits prodded like that, even if I were dead. Next time I see one, I thought, I shall bury it in the sand and put a shell on top to be a gravestone.

There was no long twilight. The sun plunged into the waves, unfurling scarlet and gold streamers into the sky behind it; and once it had gone, the colours faded to lilac, then to darkness. By the time we returned to the house, night had fallen.

* * *

'Cats!' I said, catching sight of them on the verandah. 'Why didn't you tell me? Two of them.'

'I'm sorry,' said Dad. 'I don't know how I forgot to tell you such a thing. The excitement, I suppose. This one is Fuzzy. She's one of your pampered beauties, and Ginger here might look like a fierce old tom, but he's the biggest coward this side of Suez. The joke is, we keep them to guard against snakes.' Dad laughed. 'Snakes, indeed. Fuzzy would faint and require smelling salts, and Ginger would run a mile.'

'Have we ever had any snakes? In the house?' My voice felt shaky.

'Not while I've been here. But always shake your shoes and slippers before they put them on. Make sure no nasties have crawled inside.'

'Nasties? What nasties?'

'Scorpions, for instance.'

Scorpions in my slippers? I really wished, at that moment, that I could be back in England again.

That first night, I couldn't fall asleep for a long time. I lay for a while in bed under the white veils of my mosquito net, looking at the outlines of everyday things blurred by darkness and the misty walls of my small tent. I heard my mother turning out the lights in the lounge, and soon there was only a faint yellow glow from the half-open door of my parents' bedroom. The night was loud with insect noises, the sound of a million unseen wings in the long grass under the house and in the black shapes of the trees behind it. The Jameses had the radio or the gramophone turned up very loud. Their house was quite far away, yet I could hear the music plainly and even some of the words. Later, I was to learn that song by heart:

> *'I'll see you again,*
> *Whenever spring breaks through again,*
> *Time may lie heavy between*
> *But what has been*
> *Is past forgetting . . .'*

It was Mrs James's favourite, and she played it over and over again, until it was worn and scratched and thin-sounding even at its loudest.

I got out of bed very carefully, squeezing myself out of a tiny hole between the net and the bed, and I made sure to tuck the folds in after me, frightened that some dreadful creature would fly in while I was at the window. I looked across the compound to the Jameses' house. Their curtains were not drawn. Mr James must have been reading in bed, I thought, because the light was on in the bedroom. I could see the top half of a mosquito net and nothing else. Mrs James was in the lounge, standing at the window and swaying, almost dancing, in time to the music. The lamp must have been directly behind her, because her face was in darkness and her hair was lit up into a fuzzy golden halo. When the song ended and she disappeared, I thought that maybe she had gone to bed to read a little with Mr James, but she came back to the window again.

'. . . Though my life may go awry
In my heart will ever lie
Just the echo of a sigh,
Goodbye . . .'

She blew a kiss into the darkness and waved. I moved away quickly. Had she seen me? No, she couldn't have, for our house was in complete darkness. Was there someone outside? I hadn't seen anyone. After a while, I went back to the window. The music had stopped and Mr James had turned out the bedroom light, but she was on the verandah now, sitting on the wide railing, simply sitting still and looking straight ahead of her into the night. I was glad when she finally got up and went to bed. She must have slipped under the net in the dark. Perhaps her husband was a light sleeper, and she didn't want to wake him.

After the lights went out at the Jameses', I watched the night for a few moments. No street lights, no car headlights, no moon, only the light from stars to show the outlines of houses, trees and the towering mountain in the distance. Everyone must be asleep now, I thought, everyone except me. I felt quite proud of being awake longer than anyone else, until I saw a tiny square of light high up somewhere in the black hills, and seeing it shining there all alone made me feel sad. I didn't know why. I hadn't noticed it before, and I wondered who lived there. Had it been there before? How could I have missed it, if it had? Could I have mistaken it for a star?

*   *   *

26

I crawled back into bed, and just before I fell asleep, it came to me that perhaps the reason I hadn't seen the light was that someone had only just switched it on. Everywhere everyone had gone to sleep, and yet there, high up on the hill, someone was awake. Maybe they had come home late after a party, maybe a child was ill, maybe – anything at all. Safe under the net again, I thought: 'I must find out who lives there,' and then I fell asleep.

I am remembering more and more as I write. It's like holding a candle as you go into a dark room. At first, all you can see is the small, illuminated circle just around you, but gradually, as your eyes grow used to the dimness, you perceive dark shapes of things, and you recognize them, and as you walk towards them, you see them more and more clearly, every detail outlined in the golden light. I find I can even remember dreams I had then.

In the evenings, the White Room looks a little better. The light overhead and also the one beside my bed turn the walls and the woodwork pale yellow, and there are entertaining shadows in the corner near the chest of drawers and on the ceiling. Outside, there is darkness and rain and the sound of the sea. I can hear the rain against the glass, like a spray of tiny stones. If someone were standing on the hockey pitch at this moment, they could look up here and wonder what was going on, who was imprisoned in the room behind my curtains, in the warm light. What a lot of nonsense! Who on earth could possibly be out on a night like this, and why should they even look up? But if, if . . . then they could imagine themselves a whole drama, if they wanted to. That's the glory of windows at night.

I have always (or perhaps only since that first night in Borneo) been drawn to lighted windows. If the curtains are pulled across, you are free to invent what's behind them, and if they are open, then shadows glimpsed, faces, sounds, movements caught sight of in an instant, can form a sequence, a story that may bear no relation to the truth, and in spite of that – or maybe because of it – fill the mind with pleasurable fancies.

It was bitterly cold the night my parents first brought me to this school, nearly seven years ago. The buildings rose out of a mist of falling snow, black against a dark grey sky, huge, horrifying. But set into the black mass were hundreds of small, golden window-squares, glowing and winking, and I thought of toasted crumpets in front of study fires, heads bent over neat homework, and rooms filled with books in leather bindings.

Oh, yes, I'd read all the school stories I could lay my hands on, and now the images of life behind those windows comforted me, and covered up for a little while the sick feeling in my stomach, and I pushed back the tears that had been waiting all day behind my eyes.

Windows at night are deceptive. Nothing is the same once you have found yourself on the other side of the glass. The mystery, the glamour, the romance is gone, and there you are in a world that is only the real world, after all. It's better to see things by daylight for the first time. That's how I first saw the Club in Borneo – in bright sunlight that showed up the scuffed floors, the tatty armchairs and the tables stained with rings of moisture from the bottoms of glasses emptied years and years ago. If I'd seen it first on a Saturday night from the bottom of the hill, with fairy lights strung along the roof and music and laughter pouring out of the windows, then I'd have thought it was palace of dreams and happiness, which wouldn't have been quite true. I think, even then, I knew that people went there to be together because they were far away from home and needed to talk to other people who knew what it felt like. They went to keep in touch with something they had lost, for the moment. They made cheerful noises, and I daresay if you'd asked anyone if they missed England, they would have laughed in your face. Still, the newspapers and magazines were read over and over again, and not just for the news. They were already weeks out of date by the time they reached Jesselton.

2

Cook was cutting up the pawpaw for breakfast with an evil-looking knife, curved a little, like a pirate's. He smiled at me when I came into the kitchen and nodded at the fruit.

'Take,' he said. 'Okay.'

So I took a piece and began to eat it.

I'd had pawpaw before, in the hotel in Singapore. It's a funny fruit, shaped like a melon, with pinky-orange flesh. It's good with the juice of a fresh lime squeezed on it, first thing in the morning.

I stood by the table. Amah came in to fetch the plates, and she was smiling. What was her real name? Hers and Cook's? Now was the time to ask, I thought. I'd do it now.

I said: 'Good morning. Will you tell me your real name?'

'Amah,' said Amah, pointing at herself, 'and Cook.' She pointed carefully at him.

'No,' I said. 'I know you're amah and he's the cook,

30

but what's your name, your real name? My name is
Flora.'

'Missee Flora,' said Amah.

I felt embarrassed. 'Not Missee. Just Flora.'

'Missee Flora is good manners,' said Amah.

'But Flora's friendlier, isn't it? Otherwise I shall feel
like one of those dreadful children in an old-
fashioned book, who has a nanny or a governess or
something . . .' I blushed, realizing that neither Cook
nor Amah understood what I was saying. I took a deep
breath.

'I'm sorry. I'm talking too much. But please call me
Flora.'

'Flora,' they both said.

'And I wish you'd tell me your names. Can I call you
by your proper names?'

'Okay,' said Cook. 'Okay.' He stabbed a finger into
his chest. 'Shau Yee.'

'Kuta,' said Amah, and half curtsied as she said it.

'Thank you,' I said. 'Will you teach me how to say
things in Malay?'

'Yes,' said Kuta. 'Chakap – talk. Bagus – good.'

I smiled. I'd just thought of something.

'How do you say "a lot, too much"?'

'Banyak,' said Kuta.

I pointed at myself. 'Chakap banyak,' I said, with
some pride. Shau Yee and Kuta laughed and clapped.

Dad came in to see what the noise was about.

'Good girl, Tuan,' said Kuta. 'Flora is good girl.'

'Really?' Dad looked at Shau Yee, still chortling to

31

himself as he wiped his cutlass. 'You amaze me. Come on, Flora, come and have breakfast now. Your mother wishes to look around the Fortnum and Mason's of North Borneo.

Huat Lee's was full of everything anyone could possibly want: cosmetics, toys, Chinese herbs and spices in glass jars, handbags, stockings, jewellery, tinned foods (even milk in tins), drinks, chocolate, fish, material for dresses. I knew Mum would look at every single thing, probably twice over, so I sat on a wooden crate, feeling bored and eating the Crunchie bar Mr Huat Lee (or Huat? Or Lee? I couldn't remember what I was supposed to call him) had given me, to mark my first visit to his shop. I thought it was very kind of him. Nobody in England gave you bars of chocolate for coming into their shop.

It was very hot. The crate I was sitting on was as far away from the door, and as near to a fan, as possible. I tried to make the Crunchie last as long as I could, but the chocolate was all melted and sticky and oozing out of its wrapping, so I popped the last piece in my mouth, and when that was gone, I began to lick my fingers.

'Is it tasty?' someone said.

I looked around to see who was talking to me, and there was an old man sitting just inside the doorway of a small back room. A game of chess was set out on a little table beside him.

'Yes, thank you, lovely,' I said.

'You play chess, perhaps?'

all the shiny, loose, golden hair that I had seen in the night was plaited up into a coil at the back of her neck, like a golden sea-serpent asleep, with glittering scales. Greeny-gold. She was very pale. All the other ladies were brown, or pink, or freckled or red-faced, but Mrs James was creamy-white, as though she never went out at all. Some ladies wore frocks (pale colours, or flowers), some wore skirts, gathered at the waist, and short-sleeved blouses, some were in tennis clothes, some in slacks. Mrs James wore a straight black cotton dress with a high collar, in the Chinese style.

I sat down and looked at everything and listened to the scraps of talk floating around the room . . . 'the trouble with her is she won't admit she's not living in South Kensington . . . They never do. They run amok every month or so. It's only to be expected . . . not more than half a day off a week, otherwise, they get spoiled . . . like children, really . . . need discipline . . . they're junior to us, and yet there she was, not next to the Governor, but the next one down, and flirting with poor MacIntosh, would you believe it? . . . having exams, soon, poor things, and counting the days till the summer holidays . . . well, of course, I miss them, but what can you do? They have to be educated, after all . . . get so red when they first go in the sun, poor darlings . . . I always boil and filter my water . . . can't be too careful . . . new lot of tinned stuff . . . from Australia . . . Huat Lee's keeping me a dozen . . .'

I got bored very quickly, even with the bits that I could understand.

* * *

He spoke English with a foreign accent, but I didn't think it was polite to ask him where he came from. His hair was white and very thin. I could see the pink scalp underneath.

'No,' I answered, 'but I can play checkers. Chess looks much nicer. I like the pieces, especially the horses. Are they made of ivory?'

'Yes, ivory, and ebony the black. They are called knights. And this is the queen. These are bishops, rooks, pawns. And, of course, the king.'

'It's like a play,' I said.

I was thinking: real ivory, like in the poem about ivory, apes and peacocks, sandalwood and cedar wood. Mum had bought a sandalwood chest in Singapore. It smelled sharp and spicy and dusty at the same time.

'Yes,' said the man after a while. 'It is like a war. It is a struggle for power.'

I said: 'Who are you playing with?' The man smiled.

'Today,' he said, 'I am not playing. I am considering a problem.'

'Oh,' I said. 'Like a sum in school, do you mean?'

'Like that, yes. I have to see what is best to be done in this situation. You forgive me if I return to it now.' He bent his head over the board again and began to sing softly to himself.

'Here you are, Flora,' said Dad suddenly. 'We're ready to go now. Have you been bored stiff?'

'No, I've been talking about chess to an old gentleman.'

'Oh, is he here?' Dad said. 'Come on.' He took my hand. Mum was already standing at the door. Then he said: 'I shouldn't, by the way, mention to your mother that you were chatting to that old man.'

'Why? Who is he? He seemed so nice. What's wrong with him?'

'Calm down, for goodness sake. One question at a time. I forget his name. I did know it, I'm sure someone told me, but it doesn't matter. I'm also sure he's nice, but the thing is, he's a little strange.'

'Mad, do you mean?' I could hardly believe it.

'No, no, nothing like that. Just a little eccentric, perhaps. I mean, don't you think it's a little odd, sitting in Huat Lee's back room, playing chess?'

I didn't, so I said nothing. Dad went on: 'Anyway, better not say anything to your mother.'

'Okay, I won't,' I said. 'Can we go to the Club now, please?'

The car seats were hot and burned the backs of my legs as I sat down. By the time we drove up to the Club I'd forgotten all about the old man.

The Recreation Club, always called the Club, was a pleasant, white-painted building standing at the top of a little hill. At the bottom of the hill was the Padang, the wide field used for police parades, cricket matches, school sports days and processions of all kinds. As we arrived, the police band was marching round it, small figures dressed in khaki, playing 'Colonel Bogey' on shiny brass instruments. were beds of oleander and hibiscus around the ing, and flame-of-the-forest trees made shadows on the red roof.

'Why?' I asked. 'Why does everybody go to th on Saturday morning?'

'To start the weekend with a nice cheerful ch their friends,' said Dad. 'To have a cool drink a that hot shopping, to read the *Illustrated Londc* and *Punch* and so on. A month or two out of da still. Just to have fun.'

'Do a lot of children go?'

Dad thought for a while. 'Not a lot, no. I si they're all busy with Cubs and Brownies and sc I don't expect you'll go much after you get t everyone at school on Monday. Mrs Aston teacher, might be here. I'll introduce you, if sh

'Are you sure,' asked Mum, 'that no one dre on Saturday morning?' She took out a p compact. 'Just let me do my nose again before out. This climate, honestly! Five minutes after y the powder on, it's disappeared and there you a a nose like a mirror!'

Mrs Aston wasn't at the Club. 'Such a pity Mum, but I felt quite relieved. Dad pointed o James and her husband, sitting on high stools bar. I thought: that means that dancing classes on Saturday morning. I hope Dad remembers t I can go. Mrs James was quite old and very thi

* * *

I felt a little lonely, marooned on my island of chair in a wide sea of floor, and hoped my parents hadn't forgotten all about me. They were talking to some people sitting at a table a few yards away. I wondered if I could go and ask the man at the next table for the *Punch* he'd just put down, but I didn't in the end, because I wasn't sure whether it was the done thing. Directly above me, a huge, three-bladed fan like an aeroplane propellor went round and round with a noise like the click and whirr of an enormous insect. There was a smaller fan on the bar, which buzzed as it turned this way and that, moving the air a little as it went. Men were laughing, showing their teeth a lot, shouting for more drinks; and the white-suited waiters, who moved in and out of the knots of people, were called 'boy', even though none of them were boys at all, but men, and really quite old men, some of them. I wouldn't answer, I thought, I just wouldn't. We had a teacher like that, once. 'You . . .' she used to say, 'you . . . that girl there . . .' just because she couldn't be bothered to remember our names. She didn't think we were worth it. This was the same sort of thing.

'Hello,' said a voice just behind me. 'Are you all by yourself?' I turned in my chair and saw the little girl I'd seen yesterday from the car window. I was sure it was her.

'No,' I said. 'My parents are here. They're over there.'

37

'They don't look as if they're coming back very soon. May I talk to you?'

'Yes, I suppose so,' I said. 'How old are you?'

'Eight. I usually say nearly nine, but really it's eight.'

I thought: she's only a baby, I can't get friendly with her. I'll be ten soon. Well, quite soon. Whatever shall we talk about? I said, 'I'm nearly ten.'

'You'll be with the big ones, then. At school, I mean. Are you coming to our school? Mrs Aston's?'

'Yes. I didn't know there were any others.'

'There are a couple, but ours is nicest. You'll be with Chris and Eileen and Bob and Steve and Tony. I don't expect you'll ever speak to me.'

'I shall if I feel like it. I don't know your name.'

'I know who you are. Flora Baxter. I'm Vinnie.' The girl pulled a chair away from another table and sat down next to me.

'Vinnie,' I said. 'Is that short for something?'

'Yes, but I'll only tell you if you swear not to laugh.'

'I swear.'

'Come on, then,' said Vinnie. 'I'll whisper.'

She leaned over and breathed right in my ear: 'Lavinia.'

'That's not funny. It's jolly pretty, I think.'

'Not if it's shortened to "Lav" or "Lavvy" or even "Lavatory Brush"! That's what Tony called me when he first came, then I kicked him very hard on the legs, and he stopped. He only calls me that sometimes now.'

'I get called "Flossie," or "Flo" or "Floribunda." It's awful.'

38

but what's your name, your real name? My name is Flora.'

'Missee Flora,' said Amah.

I felt embarrassed. 'Not Missee. Just Flora.'

'Missee Flora is good manners,' said Amah.

'But Flora's friendlier, isn't it? Otherwise I shall feel like one of those dreadful children in an old-fashioned book, who has a nanny or a governess or something . . .' I blushed, realizing that neither Cook nor Amah understood what I was saying. I took a deep breath.

'I'm sorry. I'm talking too much. But please call me Flora.'

'Flora,' they both said.

'And I wish you'd tell me your names. Can I call you by your proper names?'

'Okay,' said Cook. 'Okay.' He stabbed a finger into his chest. 'Shau Yee.'

'Kuta,' said Amah, and half curtsied as she said it.

'Thank you,' I said. 'Will you teach me how to say things in Malay?'

'Yes,' said Kuta. 'Chakap – talk. Bagus – good.'

I smiled. I'd just thought of something.

'How do you say "a lot, too much"?'

'Banyak,' said Kuta.

I pointed at myself. 'Chakap banyak,' I said, with some pride. Shau Yee and Kuta laughed and clapped.

Dad came in to see what the noise was about.

'Good girl, Tuan,' said Kuta. 'Flora is good girl.'

'Really?' Dad looked at Shau Yee, still chortling to

himself as he wiped his cutlass. 'You amaze me. Come on, Flora, come and have breakfast now. Your mother wishes to look around the Fortnum and Mason's of North Borneo.

Huat Lee's was full of everything anyone could possibly want: cosmetics, toys, Chinese herbs and spices in glass jars, handbags, stockings, jewellery, tinned foods (even milk in tins), drinks, chocolate, fish, material for dresses. I knew Mum would look at every single thing, probably twice over, so I sat on a wooden crate, feeling bored and eating the Crunchie bar Mr Huat Lee (or Huat? Or Lee? I couldn't remember what I was supposed to call him) had given me, to mark my first visit to his shop. I thought it was very kind of him. Nobody in England gave you bars of chocolate for coming into their shop.

It was very hot. The crate I was sitting on was as far away from the door, and as near to a fan, as possible. I tried to make the Crunchie last as long as I could, but the chocolate was all melted and sticky and oozing out of its wrapping, so I popped the last piece in my mouth, and when that was gone, I began to lick my fingers.

'Is it tasty?' someone said.

I looked around to see who was talking to me, and there was an old man sitting just inside the doorway of a small back room. A game of chess was set out on a little table beside him.

'Yes, thank you, lovely,' I said.

'You play chess, perhaps?'

* * *

He spoke English with a foreign accent, but I didn't think it was polite to ask him where he came from. His hair was white and very thin. I could see the pink scalp underneath.

'No,' I answered, 'but I can play checkers. Chess looks much nicer. I like the pieces, especially the horses. Are they made of ivory?'

'Yes, ivory, and ebony the black. They are called knights. And this is the queen. These are bishops, rooks, pawns. And, of course, the king.'

'It's like a play,' I said.

I was thinking: real ivory, like in the poem about ivory, apes and peacocks, sandalwood and cedar wood. Mum had bought a sandalwood chest in Singapore. It smelled sharp and spicy and dusty at the same time.

'Yes,' said the man after a while. 'It is like a war. It is a struggle for power.'

I said: 'Who are you playing with?' The man smiled.

'Today,' he said, 'I am not playing. I am considering a problem.'

'Oh,' I said. 'Like a sum in school, do you mean?'

'Like that, yes. I have to see what is best to be done in this situation. You forgive me if I return to it now.' He bent his head over the board again and began to sing softly to himself.

'Here you are, Flora,' said Dad suddenly. 'We're ready to go now. Have you been bored stiff?'

'No, I've been talking about chess to an old gentleman.'

'Oh, is he here?' Dad said. 'Come on.' He took my hand. Mum was already standing at the door. Then he said: 'I shouldn't, by the way, mention to your mother that you were chatting to that old man.'

'Why? Who is he? He seemed so nice. What's wrong with him?'

'Calm down, for goodness sake. One question at a time. I forget his name. I did know it, I'm sure someone told me, but it doesn't matter. I'm also sure he's nice, but the thing is, he's a little strange.'

'Mad, do you mean?' I could hardly believe it.

'No, no, nothing like that. Just a little eccentric, perhaps. I mean, don't you think it's a little odd, sitting in Huat Lee's back room, playing chess?'

I didn't, so I said nothing. Dad went on: 'Anyway, better not say anything to your mother.'

'Okay, I won't,' I said. 'Can we go to the Club now, please?'

The car seats were hot and burned the backs of my legs as I sat down. By the time we drove up to the Club I'd forgotten all about the old man.

The Recreation Club, always called the Club, was a pleasant, white-painted building standing at the top of a little hill. At the bottom of the hill was the Padang, the wide field used for police parades, cricket matches, school sports days and processions of all kinds. As we arrived, the police band was marching round it, small figures dressed in khaki, playing

34

'Colonel Bogey' on shiny brass instruments. There were beds of oleander and hibiscus around the building, and flame-of-the-forest trees made zig-zag shadows on the red roof.

'Why?' I asked. 'Why does everybody go to the Club on Saturday morning?'

'To start the weekend with a nice cheerful chat with their friends,' said Dad. 'To have a cool drink after all that hot shopping, to read the *Illustrated London News* and *Punch* and so on. A month or two out of date, but still. Just to have fun.'

'Do a lot of children go?'

Dad thought for a while. 'Not a lot, no. I suppose they're all busy with Cubs and Brownies and so forth. I don't expect you'll go much after you get to know everyone at school on Monday. Mrs Aston, your teacher, might be here. I'll introduce you, if she is.'

'Are you sure,' asked Mum, 'that no one dresses up on Saturday morning?' She took out a powder compact. 'Just let me do my nose again before we get out. This climate, honestly! Five minutes after you put the powder on, it's disappeared and there you are with a nose like a mirror!'

Mrs Aston wasn't at the Club. 'Such a pity!' said Mum, but I felt quite relieved. Dad pointed out Mrs James and her husband, sitting on high stools at the bar. I thought: that means that dancing classes aren't on Saturday morning. I hope Dad remembers to ask if I can go. Mrs James was quite old and very thin, and all the shiny, loose, golden hair that I had seen in the night was plaited up into a coil at the back of her neck, like a golden sea-serpent asleep, with glittering scales. Greeny-gold. She was very pale. All the other ladies were brown, or pink, or freckled or red-faced, but Mrs James was creamy-white, as though she never went out at all. Some ladies wore frocks (pale colours, or flowers), some wore skirts, gathered at the waist, and short-sleeved blouses, some were in tennis clothes, some in slacks. Mrs James wore a straight black cotton dress with a high collar, in the Chinese style.

I sat down and looked at everything and listened to the scraps of talk floating around the room . . . 'the trouble with her is she won't admit she's not living in South Kensington . . . They never do. They run amok every month or so. It's only to be expected . . . not more than half a day off a week, otherwise, they get spoiled . . . like children, really . . . need discipline . . . they're junior to us, and yet there she was, not next to the Governor, but the next one down, and flirting with poor MacIntosh, would you believe it? . . . having exams, soon, poor things, and counting the days till the summer holidays . . . well, of course, I miss them, but what can you do? They have to be educated, after all . . . get so red when they first go in the sun, poor darlings . . . I always boil and filter my water . . . can't be too careful . . . new lot of tinned stuff . . . from Australia . . . Huat Lee's keeping me a dozen . . .'

I got bored very quickly, even with the bits that I could understand.

* * *

I felt a little lonely, marooned on my island of chair in a wide sea of floor, and hoped my parents hadn't forgotten all about me. They were talking to some people sitting at a table a few yards away. I wondered if I could go and ask the man at the next table for the *Punch* he'd just put down, but I didn't in the end, because I wasn't sure whether it was the done thing. Directly above me, a huge, three-bladed fan like an aeroplane propellor went round and round with a noise like the click and whirr of an enormous insect. There was a smaller fan on the bar, which buzzed as it turned this way and that, moving the air a little as it went. Men were laughing, showing their teeth a lot, shouting for more drinks; and the white-suited waiters, who moved in and out of the knots of people, were called 'boy', even though none of them were boys at all, but men, and really quite old men, some of them. I wouldn't answer, I thought, I just wouldn't. We had a teacher like that, once. 'You . . .' she used to say, 'you . . . that girl there . . .' just because she couldn't be bothered to remember our names. She didn't think we were worth it. This was the same sort of thing.

'Hello,' said a voice just behind me. 'Are you all by yourself?' I turned in my chair and saw the little girl I'd seen yesterday from the car window. I was sure it was her.

'No,' I said. 'My parents are here. They're over there.'

'They don't look as if they're coming back very soon. May I talk to you?'

'Yes, I suppose so,' I said. 'How old are you?'

'Eight. I usually say nearly nine, but really it's eight.'

I thought: she's only a baby, I can't get friendly with her. I'll be ten soon. Well, quite soon. Whatever shall we talk about? I said, 'I'm nearly ten.'

'You'll be with the big ones, then. At school, I mean. Are you coming to our school? Mrs Aston's?'

'Yes. I didn't know there were any others.'

'There are a couple, but ours is nicest. You'll be with Chris and Eileen and Bob and Steve and Tony. I don't expect you'll ever speak to me.'

'I shall if I feel like it. I don't know your name.'

'I know who you are. Flora Baxter. I'm Vinnie.' The girl pulled a chair away from another table and sat down next to me.

'Vinnie,' I said. 'Is that short for something?'

'Yes, but I'll only tell you if you swear not to laugh.'

'I swear.'

'Come on, then,' said Vinnie. 'I'll whisper.'

She leaned over and breathed right in my ear: 'Lavinia.'

'That's not funny. It's jolly pretty, I think.'

'Not if it's shortened to "Lav" or "Lavvy" or even "Lavatory Brush"! That's what Tony called me when he first came, then I kicked him very hard on the legs, and he stopped. He only calls me that sometimes now.'

'I get called "Flossie," or "Flo" or "Floribunda." It's awful.'

38

'Not as bad as a Lavatory Brush. Or Lavvy Paper. Sometimes it's Lavvy Paper. I forgot. Anyway, I hit anyone who doesn't call me Vinnie, so now they do.'

'Do you hit the big boys?' I was impressed. Vinnie was thin and small for her age.

'No.' She grinned suddenly. 'I bite them. I've got sharp teeth, you see.'

'I'd never dare.' I was giggling by now.

'Sometimes you've just got to,' said Vinnie.

'There aren't any other children here,' I said. 'Why are you here?'

'I came to see you.' Vinnie blushed. 'Well, we live on the other side of the Jameses. I can see the lights of your house from my bathroom. Daddy said you'd probably be here today, because it's your first day, so I came, too. The big ones never come to the Club except for Sports Day and things like that.'

'Aren't there any other little ones?'

'Yes,' said Vinnie, 'but they're babies. Boring, really. You can't talk to them properly about anything. But you seem nice, and you're small for your age, so I don't feel all that much younger.'

I didn't like being reminded of my size, so I changed the subject quickly.

'Do you go to dancing class?'

'Yes,' said Vinnie. 'Are you going to come? Mrs James is a very good teacher. She used to be a real dancer once. In England. I've seen the dress she wore. She took it out once, to show us. And her ballet shoes: that kind with hard toes.'

'Do any of the big children go to dancing class?'

'Well, Eileen Perkins likes coming. She likes showing off, that's why. Chris Winters comes, but only because her mum makes her. Mrs Winters is trying to turn Chris into a lady, but Chris wants to be a boy. And she always calls me Vinnie now, since I started calling her Christine. She hates that.'

'I'd like to come.'

'Then let's go and talk to Mrs James.'

'Oh, I couldn't . . .' I shrank back into my chair.

'Why not? I'll tell her who you are. She's your neighbour, for goodness sake. What are you being so shy about?'

'I don't know. Only I think I'd better wait for Mum and Dad to introduce me and ask if I can go to dancing and all that.'

Vinnie shrugged. 'All right. If you like. But she's ever so nice. She won't eat you.'

'I never thought she would. It's just . . .'

'You're shy.'

'I'm *not* shy.' I was quite angry. 'It's just that my dad said he would ask her and . . .'

'Too late now,' said Vinnie. 'She's coming over. She's coming to talk to me.'

Vinnie ran to meet Mrs James who, to my horror, did seem to be making straight for my chair. They danced a few steps together on the shiny floor, and a small group of people clapped. Vinnie curtsied. She actually curtsied, and Mrs James blew a kiss at them, just as she had blown a kiss into the dark garden last night. How could Vinnie do that? How did she dare? In front of all those people?

'This is Flora Baxter,' said Vinnie, pulling Mrs James by the hand. 'She wants to come to dancing class.'

I couldn't think of anything to say, so I stood up and began examining my sandals, marvelling at how the holes were punched into the leather to make a flower pattern.

'Hello, Flora,' said Mrs James. 'Don't be shy. We're neighbours. You won't have far to come to dancing class every Wednesday afternoon. Just across the road.'

'May I really come?' I said.

'Of course.' Mrs James smiled, and I looked up and saw that her eyes were all different colours of blue and green mixed together, like the sea. She went on: 'I look forward to seeing you. I'll go and tell your parents that I've met you. I must say hello to your mother.' She ruffled Vinnie's short yellow hair. 'Goodbye.'

Vinnie and I sat down again.

Vinnie said, 'When she unpins her hair, it's so long that she can sit on it. She showed us once. Her name is Lily. I think it suits her. She's so white.'

'Doesn't she ever swim?'

'Only in the evening. At sunset. She says the sun is bad for the complexion. She wears a big straw hat for shopping. And sunglasses.'

'There you are,' said Mum, just as though I'd been the one who had disappeared and had now returned. 'I see you've met Miss Wentworth.'

41

'Vinnie, you mean? Yes,' I said, 'and Mrs James.'

'Can Flora come to play one day?' Vinnie asked.

'Yes, of course,' said Mum, 'and you must come over to play at our house, too.'

'Thanks,' said Vinnie. 'I'd like that. I'll see you at school on Monday, Flora, though you probably won't even speak to me.'

'Of course I will,' I said. 'Why ever shouldn't I?'

'You'll see,' said Vinnie. 'All the big ones keep to themselves. They think they're very grand. I don't care. You can talk to me after school, can't you? Bye.' She waved at us, and ran across the room to find her father.

'What a nice child,' said Mum, 'and just about your age, too.'

'She's miles and miles younger than me,' I said. 'She's only eight.'

'Only eight?' said Mum. 'Fancy that! She seems very old for her age.'

'It's being so much with adults,' said Dad. 'She's an only child.'

I said: 'I'm an only child, too. And I'm with adults. Why aren't I old for my age?'

'You are in some ways,' said Mum.

Not in the ways that help very much, I thought. I said: 'But she is nice. And brave.'

'Brave?' said Dad. 'How do you know?'

'She bites boys,' I answered, wondering if I would ever be desperate enough to do such a thing myself.

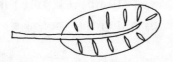

My poached egg looked distinctly pallid and reproach-ful this morning, all wispy white tendrils floating on the toast. I ate it with my eyes closed because I was hungry, but it slid down like sea-creatures. Perhaps I should stop describing tropical fruits.

Mrs James was one of the few people who looked as interesting in the daylight and close-up as she did from a distance and through a lighted window at night. Poor Miss Cornwell! She taught dancing here until last year, and when I first saw her I can remem-ber staring and wondering how such a person (beaky, dumpy, grey-haired, given to wearing purple serge with a cameo brooch at the neck) could even think about dancing, let alone teach it. There were rumours about her. A lover killed in the war. Some said, unkindly, the Boer War. But she was a good teacher, and why should she not have been? The way you look, the way you *are* when you are not dancing is un-important. Miss Cornwell, wherever you are, I'm sorry for laughing at your big bottom, along with everybody else. Perhaps you, too, before you grew old, had green-gold hair that hung down your back? Mrs James will become old one day, and her joints will stiffen, too. People may laugh at her. It's hard to imagine. I wonder where she is? I wonder if Mum and Dad ever have news of her? I should ask, but I'm a little afraid to know. Better to remember her as she was then.

And Vinnie. She's at school in England too, has been for years, like me. She's seventeen, I suppose. I haven't seen her for ages. To tell the truth, I haven't thought of her for ages. I can't imagine her in uniform, pork pie hat, tie, brown lace-up shoes, sitting with a pale face in a brown classroom. Sunny, sunburnt Vinnie, wearing old tennis shoes and faded red shorts, sitting on the schoolhouse steps eating a pomelo; a kind of pink grapefruit, which I will not describe further because of the pangs it will cause my stomach, recovering from that egg. I think I was as nervous going into school that first day as I was the night I came here.

3

The school was not like a school at all. It was no more than a small palm-thatched hut standing on its own in a field of scrub-like grass, up on stilts like all the huts across the road. A frangipani tree grew near the steps, and its glossy, dark-green leaves made a little circle of shade on the ground. The wax-white, golden-hearted flowers spread a breath of sweetness into the air, but the smells from Kampong Aya were stronger.

My father took me to school early on my first day, but there was already a group of children sitting under the tree and no sign of a teacher anywhere. As we walked towards the children, I realized that what I was wearing was wrong. They were all in shorts and Aertex shirts and no socks at all, just sandals, and I knew very well what they would think of me in a blue-and-white-striped cotton dress and ankle socks. I should have asked Vinnie what to wear. Besides I was too pale. They all looked as if they had been doing nothing but sunbathe for months and months. My father, I could tell, was wondering what to do. He had to be at his office, but was it all right to leave me there with the others, without a teacher? A tall girl, with short reddish hair falling over her forehead so that it almost hid her eyes, solved the problem.

'Hello,' she said, running up to my father. 'Are you Mr Baxter? We've all been longing to see Flora.'

'Really,' I could tell Dad was pleased. 'Well,' (pushing me forward a little), 'here she is.'

'Hello,' said the girl. 'I'm Chris Winters.'

'Hello,' I said.

We stood for a moment, then Chris said:

'It's all right to leave Flora, Mr Baxter. Honestly. We'll look after her.' She waved in the direction of the group under the tree. 'And Mrs Aston will be here in a minute.'

'Are you sure?' My father frowned at me.

'Yes, it's fine. Do go,' I said, as bravely as I could, praying inside all the time: please, God, don't let him kiss me, not in front of all of them.

'Right,' said Dad, 'I'll see you at lunch time then. Have a good day.' He turned and waved as he walked to the car.

'Come on then,' said Chris, and walked towards the others. I started to follow her and then noticed as I looked down at my feet a centipede crawling across the white toe of my cotton sock, pink legs wriggling, shrinking and growing like a tiny concertina.

'Aren't you coming?' Chris shouted over her shoulder. I couldn't move. I felt as if all the blood had left my body, and my mouth was trembling with fear, and I was trying with all my might not to cry.

46

'There's something on my foot,' I managed to say.

'Only a centipede,' said Chris, flicking the horrible creature off with her fingers. 'What are you being such a baby about?'

Why didn't I look like that? Why wasn't I tall and pretty and unafraid? Why wasn't I Chris? Why was I me?

The others, the ones sitting under the tree, were Steve – Chris's brother – Bob and Tony Dickson, and Eileen Perkins. After they had said hello to me and stared at my dress for a while, they began to talk among themselves just as though I wasn't there at all.

'You're soppy about Mrs Aston,' said Bob.

'I am *not*,' Chris glared at him. 'You're the soppy one!'

'I'm not. I don't even specially like her.'

'You bring her mangoes from your tree, and you made me find out when her birthday is.'

Bob grinned. 'You come to school early every day just to see her kissing Ian goodbye. I call that extra soppy. I call it sloppy.'

'I don't.'

'You do.'

'We don't,' said Steve. 'We come early because Dad has to be at the office.'

'But you *do* watch them kissing, don't you?' said Bob.

'How do you know?' Chris said. 'You aren't usually here.'

'Steve told me.'

Chris shouted: 'I'll punch you, Steve Winters, till you're black and blue. How dare you tell tales on me to that big dope?'

'Oh, Chris, come on. Keep your hair on,' said Steve.

'My hair's on,' she cried, 'but yours is going to be pulled out in handfuls!'

'Shut up, both of you,' said Eileen. 'Here's Mrs Aston now.'

They all sat very still, looking across the field to where Ian Aston's car was parked.

'She *is* kissing him,' whispered Tony. 'Gosh, it's just like in the pictures.'

'He's her husband. She loves him,' said Chris. 'She told me so, so there. And stop staring, Bob and Tony. Haven't you seen anyone kissing before?'

'Not like that. Not real people,' said Bob.

'I have,' said Tony.

'Who?'

'Not saying.'

'I don't believe you,' Eileen said.

'Neither do I,' said Chris. 'You're making it up.'

'I'm not. It was in the Club, one Saturday. In that little room where they keep all the newspapers and things.'

'But who was it?' said Steve.

'Charlie Farmer and Judy Sheldon.'

'Rubbish,' said Chris. 'That's nothing. They're going to be married soon. Everyone knows that. After the Coronation.'

* * *

Mrs Aston picked her way delicately towards us through the grass in pretty, high-heeled sandals. 'Hello,' they all said. 'Hello, Mrs Aston.'

Eileen, gazing in wonder at the teacher's full-skirted floral dress, her fluffy, yellow hair and her fingernails and toenails painted dark red, said, 'You look spiffing. I mean, you really look very nice. And this is Flora, the new girl.'

'Thank you very much, Eileen.' Mrs Aston laughed in a tinkly sort of way, then turned to me. 'And you're Flora. How lovely to see you. Why don't you come inside with me and I'll show you where everything is before all the little ones arrive.'

'Thank you very much,' I said.

Mrs Aston ran daintily up the steps and unlocked the door of the hut. I followed.

Inside, the shutters were still closed, but I could see the desks in rows, and the map of the world on the far wall. Mrs Aston began to open the windows on the shady side. She talked and talked, and I just stood there.

'I expect you'll find it very different from home, dear. It's not a bad place, and you do get used to it in time, but I always tell Ian it's far too close to the right-hand edge of the map for my liking. Far too far from London. The trouble is you can't get things, d'you know what I mean? This nail varnish (it's called 'Cherries in the Snow' don't you think that's a pretty name?) comes from Singapore, and Mr Lee in the shop doesn't know when he'll have any more. And to tell you the truth, I'm sick of cheese and butter in tins from Australia. You'll see. Your mother will find the same. And as for perfume, well. French perfume is like gold here, like pure gold. Ian says, 'What's wrong with Yardley's Lavender Water,' but then men don't understand such things, do they? Now, let's think. What shall we do this morning? What about a poem? Shall we all write poems? I think so. About anything you like.'

Vinnie sat with the younger children at the front of the class. She waved at me as she came in and I waved back.

'Why are you waving at her?' said Tony. 'Are you friends with a baby?'

'She's not a baby,' I said. 'She's eight, and she lives near me. And I am friends with her.'

'You don't have to wave at her in school, though, do you? They'll call you a baby, too. They won't play with you.'

I thought: I don't care. She's my friend.

But I did care. I wanted the others to like me. I bent over my work, so that I wouldn't have to look, or not look, at anyone.

We wrote poems. The very little ones copied the alphabet from their books. There was a portrait of the new Queen on the wall. The Coronation would be in June. Mrs Aston sat at her desk and wrote a letter on crinkly blue airmail paper. Then she powdered her nose. Her powder compact was gold with coloured jewels on it.

* * *

I remember the poems. Bob's was all about pirates. Eileen's was about fairies. Vinnie had written a limerick that was quite funny, even though the last line was longer than it was supposed to be. Chris hated poems and said so, loudly. Hers was about a mountain, and it was very boring. Steve's was lovely, about the women just outside the window, walking from Kampong Aya to the market in their black flapping clothes. Tony's was about a spaceship, because he read nothing but Captain Video comics; and mine was about the sea shells on the beach, and the jellyfish. I had to read it out just like everyone else and felt myself grow pink as they all stared at me, even though Vinnie smiled encouragingly at me all the way through. Once, I heard someone giggle behind me, but I couldn't tell who it was.

At break, Eileen spoke to me.

'Does your skirt stick out when you twirl around?'

'A bit.'

'I bet if Mrs Aston twirled round, hers would stick out a lot, like Jane Powell or Debbie Reynolds in the pictures.'

'She's got a lovely powder compact,' I said.

'It's real emeralds and rubies and things. She told me.'

'Really?' I was amazed. 'She must be very rich.'

'Not really. Mr Aston is a policeman. She can't be very rich.'

'She was probably just joking,' I said. 'They're probably just bits of glass.'

'Of course they're bits of glass,' said Chris. 'Eileen believes anything.'

'I don't.'

'You do.'

'I don't.'

'Yes, you do. You even believe in fairies, don't you?'

'Not all fairies, but I do believe in my fairy.'

'Why?'

'I just do, that's all. I think she's real and she lives in my tree. She puts flowers in the hollow part and things like that.'

Chris was scornful. 'Everyone knows that fairies aren't real.'

Eileen looked as if she were about to cry, and I felt sorry for her. She wasn't exactly a friend, but she had been the first of the big children to speak to me at break, so I said something, anything, to change the subject.

'Who lives up there?' I pointed to a tall, black, two-storey house halfway up the hill.

Chris giggled: 'A werewolf.'

Steve said: 'A monster.'

Bob said: 'A vampire.'

Tony said: 'A ghost.'

Eileen said: 'A dragon,' and they all rolled about shouting with laughter when they saw that I half believed them.

'I don't believe it,' I said. 'I don't believe in those things, not any of them. You're just making it up to scare me.'

'Dragons are real,' said Bob.

'They aren't,' I answered.

'Are.'

'Aren't.'

'They may not be in England, but they are here,' said Bob. 'They're just gigantic lizardy things left over from millions of years ago, and they live up there.' He pointed to Kinabalu.

I said nothing, but secretly, fearfully, thought he might be right. The creatures were everywhere in this place. I had seen carnival masks hanging in a shop on Saturday: dragon masks with huge painted red and gold eyes and golden scales and wicked, pointed fangs in a permanently open mouth. The orchids looked like dragons, the coral forests on the sea bed were probably full of dragons squirming in the watery caves, slithering into the pink hollows of enormous shells, coiling and twisting among the driftwood on the beach. I even had a tame, bedroom sort of dragon embroidered in blue silk on the back of my dressing-gown, spiralling round and round from the hem, practically breathing fire on to the back of my neck. It was easy to believe in them, and if dragons were real here, so could vampires be, and anything else, too. Couldn't they?

After break we had geography and I drew a map of Great Britain in my book and spent a long time crayoning blue sea all around it. In the end it looked like a Britain-shaped brush, with blue bristles sticking out all over. Why did Bob's sea look so different, so neat, with not one bit of blue crossing over on to the land? I have never been able to keep the colours in their proper places: they spread into one another even though all the boundaries are clearly drawn.

The little ones were drawing pictures of pirates, some of them, and others were cutting out magazines and sticking scraps on big sheets of paper. Vinnie had a book called *First Term at Malory Towers* on her desk and was reading it with great concentration. Later, after school, I said to her: 'You never even hid it. What if Mrs Aston had caught you?'

'I'd have told her that I'd finished my work,' said Vinnie, 'which I had. But she'd never have seen. She never really looks properly.'

Mrs Aston was marking exercise books. Eileen poked me in the back with a ruler. I turned round, and she held out a piece of paper, folded over and over. A note.

The note said:

'That house is haunted. It's called the Schneider house. I don't know who lives in it (someone called Schneider I suppose), but Mum says I mustn't ever go there. I think she knows something, but she won't talk about it. I don't think there's a ghost. I think it's some kind of mad person, or maybe a lot of mad people. But my amah says there are ghosts. She says she sometimes hears them singing at night. I don't believe her, not really.'

I could see it through the window, a tall, tall house on the green hill, all by itself up there with no other house for miles around, and I knew that it was in one of its upstairs windows that I had seen a light burning, late at night.

There's a little girl in the room next door to mine, a first former suffering from measles. I went to see her this morning. There she was, in a white box of a room just like this one, sitting up in bed, looking miserable and folding the top sheet into a kind of long sausage. She had teddy bears and a rabbit in bed with her, and photographs of parents and ponies on the bedside table. She looked so little, almost a baby, and yet she's older than Chris was when I first knew her, and Chris seemed so grown-up to me then. So brave and pretty and tall. Capable of anything. I suppose it is all, as they say, relative. I don't feel much different inside now from what I did then. I still have an overdeveloped imagination, and I'm still frightened of a lot of things. But I suppose I must have changed. Eighteen is nearly grown-up, isn't it?

The trouble with Borneo was, all the children over eleven were in England at school. That made the nine- and ten-year-olds a bit too big for their boots. We all played together all the time because there was no choice. That was something peculiar to the Colonies.

But there are always bogey men. A confession. To this day, if I have to get out of bed in the dark, I look under the bed first, and when I come back, I make a flying leap for the safety of the covers because you never really know what might have got in under there while you were gone. In my first year, I had to walk the whole length of the dormitory to get to the lavatory. That wasn't so bad. There was a light on in the corridor at the end, and I just fixed my eyes on that dim little bulb and ran. But coming back was different. You were walking into the darkness, and the cubicle curtains billowed out alarmingly. (Matron believed in Open Windows) and snatched at your ankles like tormenting wraiths. Even in the safety of the bed, you couldn't completely relax. It was probably only the wind puffing out the curtain like that, but didn't it just have the shape of something? Someone? 'Watch the wall, my darling,' went a song we used to sing. And I did. I watched the wall every night for a long time before coming to the conclusion that it was better to see whatever it was that was coming to get me, and face it out. I generally slept with the blankets pulled round my head. Even now, I can't bear complete darkness or complete silence. In school, the landing lights are left on and there's very little silence, but you have to get used to creaking stairs and groaning radiators. Here in the Sanatorium after ten o'clock, there is nothing but the roaring of the sea.

* * *

I shall go on writing. Why not? Sister is probably in bed, drinking Horlicks, wearing a flannel nightgown and reading the latest number of *The Lady*. If she catches me, I shall say I've just woken up. After all, I'm practically an adult. There are girls of my age out there in the real world who already have children of their own. Sleep well, Sister! You are not one of the things that I am afraid of.

4

Somehow, whenever we played at the Dicksons', no one ever wanted to do anything at all except climb on to the garage roof. I hated it. I dreaded going to play with Bob and Tony, but how could I have admitted I was terrified? The roof was sloping, made of corrugated iron. The Dicksons' bungalow was on one side of the garage, and on the other side was a hilly mound, some way away. If you climbed along the roof of the garage and leaned over a bit, you could pick mangoes from the tree, but mangoes were not the point. There were plenty of mangoes in the market, lying around in piles. The point was being able to get on to the roof.

The first time I went to the Dicksons', everyone was there: Chris and Steve and Eileen, as well as Bob and Tony.

'There's two ways,' Bob explained. 'You can run down the hill and jump, or you can stand on the verandah and climb up one of the poles onto the roof of the house and just step across.'

'What for?' I asked.

'Well, there's mangoes on the tree.'

'They're not even ripe,' I said.

Tony said, 'They're good with soya sauce even when they're not ripe.'

I shook my head. 'I can't get up there.'

'You haven't tried,' said Bob.

'I know I can't,' I said. 'You all go.'

Chris, Steve and Eileen were sitting on the verandah steps, listening, looking. I thought, why don't they say anything? Surely Eileen can't, won't go up there? They're just staring, waiting to see what I do.

'Come on, Flora, try,' said Tony. 'Just try. You're a baby if you don't try.'

'But I can't,' I said. (Could they see the tears prickling in my eyes?)

Bob said, 'Eileen can do it. She's only a bit taller than you. I should think you could easily do it.'

'All right,' I said. 'I'll try.'

I ran down the hill. Bob had shown me the special place from which they all jumped, but when I reached it, my legs seemed to grow into the ground, the sun struck the metal roof and bounced off it and dazzled me. The faces of Steve and Chris and Eileen, upturned, swam into a blur in front of my eyes. Everyone was shouting: 'Jump, Flora. Jump! Go on. Silly Flora. Silly old lump.'

I just stood there, saying to myself: I won't cry. Whatever happens, I won't let them make me cry. The gap between the side of the hill and the garage roof seemed to grow wider and wider. The others started to chant:

> *'Silly old lump*
> *Flora can't jump!'*

over and over again, poking each other in the ribs and laughing and laughing.

In the end, I came down from the hill. I sat on the verandah steps and watched as Tony and Steve shinned up the pole, onto the roof of the bungalow, then onto the garage. Bob, Chris and Eileen jumped, almost seemed to step, from the red earth of the hill onto the corrugated silvery slope to join the others. I sat on the steps and waited. Four o'clock, I thought. I'll have to wait until four o'clock. Dad will fetch me in the car. It's hours away. I began to count the seconds.

For dancing class, Mrs James wore a short tunic-like dress with no sleeves, and black ballet shoes. I wished I could have worn my pink ballet shoes with the tiny bows on the front, but I was told to take them off when I arrived with Vinnie.

'For now, dear,' Mrs James said. 'I like to see your toes. Check up on what they're doing.'

I was glad I'd asked Vinnie what to wear. My short circular skirt and white blouse were almost identical to what the others were wearing. The chairs in the Jameses' lounge had all been pushed out on to the verandah, and we took turns using the sideboard as a barre.

'It's just the right height, you see,' Mrs James explained.

'Bend-two-three, stretch-two-three, lean-two-three, up-two-three, bend-two-three, hands, Eileen, always remember your hands, dear, good, splendid and up-two-three. Rest. Good.' Mrs James still looked almost cool, even after all the loosening-up exercises.

Arms and legs came first.

'Shake them, bend them, relax all the way along your arms, no bones at all, anybody,' said Mrs James, walking along the rows in time to the music, picking up arms and hands and flopping them about to see if they were loose. After the arms, the legs and feet had a turn, stretching and pointing, lifting and bending.

'No castanets now,' said Mrs James, and everyone laughed. 'I'm sorry, Flora, you don't know what I mean, do you? Shall I tell her our awful secret?' Everyone nodded, and Mrs James went on. 'Well, when I started this class everyone was so stiff that during the pliés you could hardly hear the music for the noise of creaking and cracking joints. It really sounded like castanets.'

'I expect I'm a little bit stiff,' I said. 'I haven't done ballet for ages.'

'Well, girls' – Mrs James smiled – 'if we hear even the whisper of a castanet, we'll know it's Flora, and forgive her because this is her first time. Right, everyone. Down, and stay, and up, and rest. Good, and again.'

* * *

After the exercises were over, we sat down on the floor. I sat next to Vinnie. Mrs James explained what we were going to do next.

'It will be like acting, a kind of mime to music. But you must remember that though you haven't been given any steps, you are still dancing. Now, I'm going to ask you to take partners, and we'll do the same mime, all of us. Chris, you and Eileen can start. No, don't groan, somebody has to begin. Come up here, and all you others, watch carefully because you can learn from one another. Now, I'll put on some music. Right. You are in a forest, quite happy at first, exploring, that's good, yes, moving about, climbing even, skipping . . . good. It's sunny in the forest . . . the birds are singing . . . you are happy . . .'

I stared and stared at Chris and Eileen. I could almost feel the shade of the forest, hear the leaves rustling, imagine myself sitting on the cool ground with tall trees above me.

'. . . Now, the night is coming, darkness is falling, can you hear it in the music? . . . and gradually, slowly, it grows dark, and with the darkness comes fear . . . it's cold . . . you're alone . . . you don't know where you are . . . lost . . . terrified . . . that's good . . . you blunder along the path and then you see it . . . a light!' I breathed a sigh of relief and shook myself. Mrs James said: 'That was very good, Chris and Eileen. Now, who's next?'

*　*　*

After the class was over, Mrs James brought in glasses of lemonade on a tray. It was delicious: cold, cloudy, with little pieces of the lemon still floating around in it with the cubes of ice. Mrs James sank into a chair.

'Eileen,' she said, 'please put "We'll gather lilacs" on the gramophone. It's such a cool song.' She told us, 'Listen to the words.' We listened.

'We'll gather lilacs in the spring again
And walk together down an English lane . . .'

'There's no spring here, alas!' Mrs James sighed. 'And as for lilacs, it's years since I saw a lilac tree. All these hibiscus and oleander and frangipani, and those dreadful vulgar lilies and orchids that look as if they're about to climb out of the basket and eat you alive – you can keep them all, as far as I'm concerned. An English garden, that's what I'd like. Cool. Shady.'

I asked, 'Why can't we grow daffodils and things like that here? Why are there no roses?'

'It's too hot for them, really. They live such a short time.' She took a sip from her lemonade. 'There used to be a proper garden in the Colony. Before the war. A Germany couple, who lived up on the hill, oh, they made such a garden. We used to have tea there, and play music, and look at the roses and the grass that seemed to be growing into a proper lawn. They even had a small pond with a fountain in the middle. A water lily grew on the pond, I remember. A pink water lily. Lovely.'

'What happened to it?' I asked. 'You make it sound as if it's not there any longer.'

'It isn't.' Mrs James smiled. 'The people who lived there . . . left it. She died, and he, well, he's moved away and keeps to himself. It's very sad, really. They were good days.'

'Where was the house?' I asked.

'There it is,' Mrs James pointed out to the side of the house. 'You can just see it.'

'But that's . . .' I stopped.

'That's what?' Chris said.

'Nothing. I didn't mean to say anything. Sorry,' I said. The others went on talking. I looked at the house, the Schneider house (Schneider was a German name), the one where I had seen the light, the house that terrified me in the night and where, a long time ago, Mrs James and her friends had drunk tea in a rose garden.

Vinnie said, 'You're not very brown yet, are you?'

'I'm a lily, like Mrs James.' I was dancing round the Wentworths' verandah dressed in an assortment of scarves, pinned together with brooches. 'Rose, Rose, I Love You' was playing loudly on the gramophone. Vinnie and I sang with the record:

> 'In a rickshaw on the street
> Or in a cabaret
> Flower of Malaya
> I cannot stay.'

I said: 'Put on "Don't Let the Stars Get in Your Eyes"!'

'In a minute,' said Vinnie. 'I want "Jambalaya" first. It's better for dancing.'

'I'm tired,' I said, and went to sit down on the wide verandah railing. 'I like playing here.'

'It's because Mum and Dad are never here.'

'Not really.'

'Yes, it is. It's fun, being able to make as much noise and mess as we like.'

'Where do they go?' I asked.

'Dad goes to the office, and Mum has about a million committees and bridge parties and tea parties and sewing parties and hospital visiting and things like that.'

'Why doesn't she ever take you?'

'I wouldn't go. I'd be bored.'

'Aren't you bored here, on your own?'

'I'm not on my own, silly. You're here.'

'But when I'm not?' I said. 'And before I come?'

'No, I talk to Ah Yin. I go to her house sometimes, round the back, and she washes my hair in coconut oil to make it shine. Have you noticed how shiny her hair is? It's the coconut oil.'

It was true. Vinnie's amah had hair that shone like glass. Perhaps one day, I thought, I'll ask her to do mine. Would mine shine like that, or does it have to be black hair?

I said: 'But aren't you frightened?'

'What of?'

'I don't know.' I thought for a moment. 'Snakes,

65

robbers, fire, just being on your own. I'm frightened of so many things.'

Vinnie said: 'I'm not. Not of snakes, and robbers wouldn't come here – there's nothing to take. I'm not frightened.'

'Not of anything?'

'Let's make a list,' said Vinnie. 'You first.'

I took a deep breath: 'The dark, storms, fires, ghosts, dragons, witches, big dogs, snakes, scorpions, the jungle, being by myself, the garage roof, other people sometimes if they're being horrible. That's all I can think of. I expect I could think of some more, only I'm too hot.'

'I expect,' said Vinnie, 'that I'd be frightened of things like ghosts if I ever saw one, only I never have. I'm not frightened of snakes because they're frightened of me. I think I'm frightened of things changing, people changing, not being the same as before. Come on, let's get a drink.'

We went into the kitchen.

'At Eileen's,' I said, 'we sit in armchairs, and the amah brings drinks on a tray.'

'Really? How posh! Do you dress up?'

'A bit. Her mother only lets us use a few things. Eileen takes the dress. There's only one. She always makes me be someone awful – Ann Miller or someone like that. I'm never Jane Powell or Esther Williams or Kathryn Grayson. Does she let you?'

'She's never asked me. I'm too babyish for her,' said Vinnie.

'She's the baby,' I said. 'She believes in fairies. Really. She showed me a letter from a fairy. She found it in a banyan tree in her garden. Don't tell her I told you. It was a deadly secret.'

'I shan't tell anyone. I expect it was her mother. Writing the note, I mean. But thanks for telling me a secret. I wish I had one to tell you, but I haven't really. D'you want a piece of pawpaw?'

I took a piece and bit into it. 'Won't you need it for breakfast tomorrow?'

'I expect there's another one somewhere.' Vinnie started eating too. 'If not, we'll have pineapple or mangoes or rambutans or something . . .'

I was looking out of the kitchen window, not listening. I said, 'I'm sorry. I didn't really hear you. What was it you said?'

'Doesn't matter,' said Vinnie. 'What are you staring at?'

'That house, up in the hills, that's the one Mrs James was talking about, where the garden used to be,' I said. 'I saw a light shining there on my first night here when I couldn't sleep. Eileen's amah says there's ghosts and mad people there. I only really think of it when I haven't got something else to think about. I suppose it's one of the things I'm afraid of.'

'Well,' said Vinnie, dripping pawpaw juice onto the window sill, 'it's never hurt me, and I've lived here for ages. It's only a house. How can a house hurt you?'

'It's not the house. It's what's in the house.'

'I don't see why someone in a house is frightening.

Anyway, I'll ask my mother. I bet she knows more than Eileen's amah. I'll ask her who lives there now. I'll tell you. It can be our secret. You must promise not to tell anyone.'

'Maybe she won't know,' I said.

'She will. She knows everybody in the whole Colony. I'll ask her. I'll tell you tomorrow.'

'I'm going to lunch at Chris's house tomorrow.'

'Monday, then,' said Vinnie.

'All right.'

'What if it's a werewolf?' I asked Fuzzy, later. She was curled up on the sofa, trying hard to fall asleep. I wouldn't let her. I just kept talking. 'Mrs Wentworth will never tell Vinnie, will she? If it's something bad, someone bad, they'll tell her a lie, some story to keep her quiet. Maybe all the grown-ups just *think* it's a person living there, and really it's a Thing, a Phantom, a Truly Terrible Spectre.' Fuzzy blinked, and licked her tail. I said, 'Why aren't you interested, anyway? Ginger always listens, very politely. I'm going to find him this minute if you don't pay attention!' Fuzzy closed her eyes until they were two tiny greenish-glowing slits in the white fur of her face.

'You're useless,' I said. 'Go to sleep.'

They've sent me back to school, even though there's nothing for me to do here. I'm sitting in the reference library now, and I can hear the shouts of all the poor unfortunates careering round the playing fields. The screams of the damned, I call it, although they are probably enjoying themselves hugely. I'm very relieved to be done with games. They always seemed to me a particularly unrefined method of torture.

Consider:
(1) Bare knees, and a high wind straight off the sea. Rain, too, quite often.
(2) Mud beneath your feet, infiltrating your shoes and squelching in your socks.
(3) A lot of hard sticks that could catch you (and did catch you) painful blows on shins, ankles, and knees.
(4) An unpredictable ball that could go anywhere, and that you had to follow, even though everyone else was chasing it, so whatever was the point in getting yourself crushed in the fray?
(5) Ordinary classmates transformed into wild-eyed viragoes, hair dishevelled, panting, shouting at you because what you were doing was wrong.
(6) Mrs Williams of the shiny eyes and healthy cheeks yelling: 'Come on, Flora. Buck up. Run,' as she passed you with a leap, pleated shorts flying and red knees flashing above navy-blue socks.

That's the winter. In the summer, there's cricket. Nothing pleasanter, nothing more evocative of hearts at peace under an English heaven than the thwack of leather on willow, or is it vice-versa? It's all right if you're wearing a straw hat with long, pink satin ribbons and sitting in the shade of an ancient tree, waiting for tea and sandwiches in the pavilion, as you watch elegant young men (fair-headed, of course, and noble-browed, every last one of them) in immaculate whites running between the wickets. It's quite another thing to be stuck out in the deep field, waiting hours for someone to send a ball in your direction, then throwing it in so badly that mid-wicket has to retrieve it, and the other side is clocking up runs at an alarming rate. Batting is even worse. There you are, minding your own business, when some demon bowler with meaty thighs bowls a red cannonball straight at you with terrifying speed, and you are supposed to play forward and hit the blasted thing, and with a straight bat, what's more. Every instinct says: 'Run away,' but that's not cricket, as the saying goes, so you make a feeble gesture in the direction of the lethal scarlet projectile and lean your body as far as possible away from it, praying very hard. Even if you hit it, your troubles aren't over. You sometimes have to run, and I've always regarded running as a complete waste of time, unless there's a bus to be caught.

It's warm in here. A pale wintery sun is shining through the window. Outside, the leafless branches are waving in a high wind, but behind glass I have the illusion of heat. In England, even on the hottest summer day, there is no heat like tropical heat, Jesselton heat as it was on the day I first went to lunch in Chris's house.

5

'You must feel the heat a lot, after England,' said Mrs Winters, waving a forkful of rice elegantly over her plate without spilling a grain. 'It's different for Christine, of course, because she was born here.'

I noticed how Chris winced at her full name. 'Really?' I said. 'I didn't know.'

'It's astounding that she survived at all,' Mrs Winters went on. 'We were all In the Bag shortly after she was born.'

'In the bag?' A picture came into my mind of Mrs Winters' leathery neck and greying curls being pushed into a giant handbag with a metal clasp.

'Prisoners of the occupying Japanese army, my dear. During the war. In prison camps. It was absolutely terrible, it really was. Darling' (to Mr Winters) 'is there any more iced water in the 'fridge? Can you ring for Cook?'

Chris and Steve said nothing. I, because I was a guest and felt I had to make conversation, said, 'The food can't have been very nice, I expect.' Mrs Winters laughed. 'Food? A ration of rice, the odd green

banana, some dried fish for a treat sometimes, un-
filtered, unboiled water – we were all permanently
hungry.'

'Did anybody . . . get ill?' I asked. I was going to say
'die' but I didn't know if it was polite to talk about
death at lunchtime.

'A great many people died . . .' Mrs Winters' tone
did not change as she spoke. It might have been a
conversation about the weather, but I noticed how
tightly she was holding her knife and how bright her
eyes were. Was she going to cry?

'Chris didn't die, though, did she, Mum?' said
Steve, and Mrs Winters smiled.

'Christine throve on everything. A natural survivor.
I suppose it was a case in those days of weakest to the
wall, and Christine has always been, I'm glad to say, a
picture of health from the day she was born. Have you
seen Christine's doll, Flora?'

Why had Mrs Winters changed the subject? I
hurried to finish my mouthful. I remembered the
doll, a rag doll, sitting on a shelf in Chris's room,
staring through the window at the sea with her pearly
button eyes. I nodded silently.

'Quite a story, about that doll,' said Mr Winters. It
was the first time he had spoken, and I turned to look
at him.

Chris and Steve were raising their eyebrows at each
other as if to say . . . 'Oh, heavens not that old tale
again,' but Mr Winters had spoken so solemnly that I

said, almost felt I had to say, as though it were the next line in a play. 'I'd love to hear it. Would you tell me?'

Mrs Winters patted her mouth with a napkin.

'Don, would you fetch the photograph? Thank you, dear.' She leaned forward in her chair and filled her glass from the water jug.

Mr Winters returned to the table with a photograph, in a gold frame that seemed far too grand for the small, torn, faded picture that it held. Mrs Winters handed it to me.

'Now, that's me. Younger, of course, by ten years and a lot thinner, but me. Does it look like me?'

'Yes,' I said. 'Yes, it does.'

'And this,' said Mrs Winters, 'is Kristina. We always laughed at the coincidence of Christine having her name.'

I looked at the photograph. It was hard to see exactly what Mrs Winters' companion was like because shadows of leaves fell across her face. Her hair seemed very fair. She was smiling.

'She looks very pretty,' I said.

Mrs Winters sighed. 'Oh dear. And they say the camera never lies. She was beautiful. Like a princess. Not that I've seen many princesses, of course, but like one imagines a princess in a fairytale. Do you know what I mean?'

I nodded.

'And she was brave. She encouraged us all . . . gave us new life. She sang beautiful songs, but in German, of course, and there were some that objected to that at first, I can tell you, because during the war the Germans and Japanese were allies. But she went on singing. 'Schubert was not a Nazi,' she would say, 'and neither am I, or what would I be doing here, so far from my home?' In the end, she won them over. Kristina had a baby, two or three months older than Christine. There were no toys or playthings in the camp, and most of the children were so weak and listless they didn't even care, much of the time. Anyway, Kristina took it into her head that she was going to make a doll for Liesel. That was her daughter's name: Liesel. I ask you, a doll under those conditions. But she tore up an old skirt and she stitched it with a needle she had managed to hide away, and she used threads pulled carefully out of skirts, shirts, sheets, anything she could find. She hoarded coloured threads like a miser and with these she embroidered the features. She scrounged from everyone, and she got lace from someone's petticoat for the trimmings of the dress, and one of the Japanese guards brought her two buttons for the eyes. Everyone helped to make that doll, gave things toward it, watched its progress, longed for it to be finished. You're probably surprised that a crowd of grown women could be so obsessed with a doll, but you see, there was nothing to do all day except think of how to get food for our children and ourselves, and the doll . . . provided an interest, something everyone could join in with. Anyway, to cut a long story short, the doll was finished at last. Then, sometime later, little Liesel died. We buried her one afternoon under the trees, and everyone wept, even one or two of the guards. Everyone except Kristina. She did not shed one tear, poor thing, but stood there clutching the doll. It would have been far better for her if she had cried. She walked away from the grave. I can see her still, walking through the dust, and she went over to where my Christine was lying on a straw mat in a patch of shade and put the doll down beside her. She closed Christine's little hand into a fist tight round the doll's hand, and then she went into the hut.'

Mrs Winters stopped speaking. No one said anything for a long moment.

I said, 'What happened to Kristina? Did she die?'

'Die?' Mrs Winters nodded. 'Not till later though. After the war. It would have been better if she had died with her child.' Mrs Winters rose from the table and smiled. 'Enough of these old stories. It was all a long time ago. Run and play now and forget about all these sad things.' She pushed her chair up to the table and left the room. I thought, Chris is only ten and a half now. I don't call that a long time ago.

We went out on to the verandah.

'What did your mother mean, Chris?' I asked, 'when she said that it would have been better if Kristina had died straight away?'

'I don't know,' said Chris. 'I've heard that story so often that I'm bored to tears by the whole thing. Probably she went mad or something. Come on. Let's go and see if Bob and Tony are coming. They said they'd come after lunch.'

'Do we have to play Cowboys again?' I said.

'There's four of us and only one of you,' said Chris, 'so you must play what we like.'

'And we like Cowboys,' said Steve.

I thought of saying that guests were usually allowed to choose the games, at least sometimes, and then I thought better of it. After all, Bob and Tony were guests, too, and they liked Cowboys and Indians. But they only came after lunch. I was the more guest-like guest. Still.

'You don't have to be a Cowboy or an Indian today.' Chris grinned. 'You're no good at running, and you can't aim a gun or throw a lasso.'

'Thanks,' I said. 'I'll just wait here till . . .'

'No, no,' said Steve. 'You're going to be a prisoner, we've decided. See, I've captured you. Me and Bob. You're a rancher's daughter. I'm going to take you and tie you up and then I'm getting ready to kill you, and Chris and Tony will ride in and rescue you.'

'What do I have to do?'

'Nothing. Just be tied up to a tree for a while. It won't hurt. I won't tie you up too tight.'

I shivered. 'Are you sure they'll come and rescue me? Is that part of the game?'

'Yes, yes,' said Tony. 'They come while we're out hunting. We'll tie you up, then go hunting, and while we're gone, they'll come and rescue you. Come on, you should be pleased. You've got the most important part.'

* * *

The Winters had a huge garden. Near the house, two gardeners had worked hard to make flowerbeds and lawns, but further away the jungle spread green creepers through the trees, the grass was long and dense, and the thick fragrance of unseen flowers hung in the air.

'We'll tie her to the coconut palm,' said Steve, dragging me by the hand into the wilderness. Bob said: 'You must scream a bit.'

I squeaked obligingly.

'That's not a scream.' Steve kicked me. 'Scream properly.' I tried, but all I could produce was a strangled wail. 'Pinch her, Bob, really hard, go on.'

'No, please.' I said.

'Yes,' said Steve, 'go on.'

'No,' I said, 'I'll scream, really I will. I promise.'

I closed my eyes and thought of all the creatures at this moment scuttling, sliding, crawling, hunching their way through the yellowish grass towards the tree, towards me, and then I opened my mouth and screamed and screamed.

'Stop!' shouted Steve. 'Stop!' The grown-ups will come running.

'You said scream.'

'I meant scream quietly, stupid. They'll think we're killing you.'

'Come on,' said Bob. 'Stand here. Right next to the tree, and I'll tie you up.'

I stood quite still as the rope was wound round and round the tree and round and round me. The sharp bark bit into my back.

'We're going now,' said Steve. 'Hunting. The others will be here in a minute.'

'Okay,' I said. 'Do I have to scream again?'

'No, they have to find you by themselves, silly. You can faint, if you like. You know, just sort of slouch.'

I nodded and wished that I really *could* faint and wake up in the Winters' lounge when it was all over.

The air just above the grass trembled in the heat, and the leaves were loud with the humming of insects. My thoughts went round and round in my head: where are they? Why can't I hear them? Talking, playing, planning my rescue? It's hot – think of snow and puddles on pavements, frost on dead leaves, November rain, darkness, and then the heat won't seem so bad. Why don't they come? I know what they're doing. They're going to see how long I can stand it before I shout for help. I'll just show them, that's all. I'll count and say poems and sing songs in my head, and I won't be scared. Whatever happens. There's nothing to be scared of, not even snakes. Snakes won't come. Vinnie says they're more frightened of me than I am of them. I wonder how she knows. I'll see her tomorrow. She's asking about the house. She'll tell me at school. Think of school. Think of tomorrow. Think of Vinnie. Dad's coming later. When? What's the time? Will I have to stay here long? Where are they? Why aren't they talking somewhere? I WILL NOT shout out. I don't care what happens. Serve them all right if something happened to me. If I got malaria from mosquito bites, or if I just died of heat. Serve them right. I started counting. I counted to a thousand. Nothing. No one. I'll start again, I decided. Why don't they come? Maybe they've really forgotten about me, forgotten I'm here at all. No, that's stupid. It's a game. They know I'm here. Oh, yes, they know. They're testing me. I won't cry. Think of the snow. Cold, white, soft, wet snow. Cold. I fainted.

'So what did you do all afternoon?' said Dad.

I said nothing for a few seconds. Better not to tell him about being tied to a tree for nearly an hour.

'We played Cowboys and Indians. They always play something like that. I hate it.'

'Why don't they ever play what you want?'

'They won't, that's all.'

'You should put your foot down and refuse to play. Assert yourself.'

'It's a bit hard when there's four of them.'

'Nonsense. It's a question of character. You just let them push you around. I can't think why.'

I didn't answer. I looked out of the car window, and blinked back tears. I haven't got a character, I thought, that's why. I'm all squishy, like that dead jellyfish. I want them to like me, so I do what they say, and they don't really like me any better. If I didn't do what they said all the time, maybe they would like me a little more. And then again, maybe they wouldn't. Maybe they simply wouldn't have anything to do with me. I daren't take the risk.

* * *

I was hot and feverish that night. A touch of sun, Mum said. All night long, I had bad dreams. I was trapped in a jungle and couldn't get out. Every time I cut away a creeper from in front of me, another sprang up in my path and curled around my ankles and plucked at my dress. Thorns and rough grasses scratched me as I tried to walk, and the sky was very low above my head, burning white. At the end, I was exactly where I had been all along. My struggles had been for nothing.

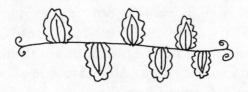

Quite often, on Sunday afternoons, especially in the Michaelmas Term, we have lectures on this and that: Stone Age remains, the manufacture of fishing hooks in seventeenth-century Iceland, up the Orinoco with rod and camera – that sort of thing. There are often slides, and someone gives a vote of thanks afterwards, and then we all go and have supper. Sometimes we have recitals, and these are much pleasanter. A plump soprano sings to us, or a pianist plays, or maybe a quartet, and while the music fills the hall, your mind can wander at will. But during this afternoon's recital, a strange thing happened – a coincidence I suppose you could call it – and it has sent me hurrying back here to my study to write. A baritone was singing, and the first half of the recital was full of unremarkable ditties about ships and the sea, and love being like all sorts of things, and so on. After the interval, I didn't even bother to look at the programme. I was miles away, worlds away when the music began, but I recognized it at once: Schubert's *Die schöne Müllerin.* I listened for a while, surprised that the songs should be so familiar to me, after so long. I hadn't heard them for eight years, and yet this afternoon when I was thinking about them, remembering how they sounded so long ago (because that was what I had been doing when I wasn't listening to our recital), there they were. It was like looking up a new word in the dictionary. After you know what it means, it seems to come up everywhere. This afternoon's pianist was a tightly corseted lady in royal blue brocade whose podgy little fingers skimmed over the keys with great speed. The baritone was thin and tall with brilliantined hair, like a smooth black-and-white bird. It didn't matter a bit. Neither did the coughing, chair-scraping and general fidgeting of over two hundred people.

The first time I heard it, I didn't know what the words meant, but the music was cool and rippled into the tropical afternoon like mountain water over stones. And today the magic was still there. The heavy, rather moth-eaten velvet curtains of the Hall, the pock-marked parquet floor and the canvas and metal chairs we all sat in vanished in the closing of my eyes, and there instead were grassy banks and flowers growing and a mill-wheel turning, lazily turning, and a stream flowing like the music itself and sparkling and circling in little whirlpools, frothing over pebbles, running transparent over a hand dipped into the water. Some of the songs were sad, the music slower, the singer's voice plaintive: dark hollows and shadows underneath the shimmering surface.

After the recital, I tried to keep the music in my head, tried to keep it with me till now. One song 'Morgengrüss' goes in and out of my thoughts as I write, and I think, maybe, that it was *this* song, this very one, I heard that afternoon in Huat Lee's shop. But I can't be sure. It could be my memory playing tricks.

6

The black figures on the page wouldn't stay still. Perhaps I wasn't quite well yet after all that sun. Monday morning, and Vinnie as usual had been late. She waved at me as she sat down and mouthed a few words. 'I'll tell you later,' I think she said. About the house, probably. I wished break would come. It was hard to concentrate. Out of the window I could see the blue and mauve mass of the mountain; voices drifted across from Kampong Aya and a dragonfly was flitting backwards and forwards across the window, backwards and forwards, unable to make up its mind whether to come in or not. There was an interesting-looking crack in the floorboards. I could see grass under the hut.

'Children,' said Mrs Aston as she collected our books, 'I have an important announcement to make.' She sounded almost efficient. 'The *Sabah Times* is holding an essay competition, and the first prize will be a Parker '51 pen and pencil set. The winning entry will be published in the newspaper. I hope a lot of you will enter, because wouldn't it be a feather in our cap if someone from this school won? You have a week until the competition closes, and I shall write the choice of subjects on the blackboard. If you bring in your entries next Monday, then I shall deliver them to the editor myself.' She turned to the board and then thought of something else and turned back to us.

'All efforts must be entirely your own work. No help from mums and dads with spelling or punctuation.' She took up chalk and began to write.

The subjects were: 'The Coronation,' 'My home,' 'Life a hundred years from now – What will it be like?' and 'The Legend of Kinabalu.' My hand was trembling as I wrote the titles down, and I knew, I knew at once that I had to write about that mountain. Kuta had told me of the dragon that lived hidden among the crags on the summit. All I would have to do would be to make up a story about it. I would invent everything. I was longing to start, to describe the clothes, the people, the dark caves, and especially the Dragon himself – oh, I could just see him: huge and silvery with eyes rimmed with fire and claws like splinters of diamond – I would win, I knew I would, I couldn't believe that pen and pencil set wouldn't be mine. I could almost see it in my satchel. I could imagine what the pen would feel like between my fingers. Why didn't the time go more quickly? I wanted to get home, I wanted to start. I'd forgotten all about the house on the hill and how much I'd been longing to hear what Vinnie had to say about it.

* * *

'Have a bit.' Vinnie tore off a large, pink segment of pomelo.

'Thanks. Have you found out about the house?'

'Yes, I have. You'll never believe it.'

'Then tell me,' I said.

'Okay.' Vinnie took a deep breath. 'Are you ready?'

'Yes,' I breathed. I was trembling a little. What was I expecting?

'Well, it's empty. It has been for years. There!' Vinnie bit into another slice of fruit.

'But . . .' I didn't know what to say. 'It isn't. I've seen a light there. Often.'

'How often?'

'Well, once or twice.'

'There you are then. You probably saw fireflies or something. They're very bright, you know.'

'No, it was a real light. I know it was.'

'Then who,' said Vinnie, 'do you think it could be? My mum says the house is empty. She told me all about it. She remembers the people who lived there, just like Mrs James. She told me about the garden, and she said that while the wife was alive the house was full of lights and music, and people used to go there for marvellous parties. Mum couldn't have made it all up.'

I said nothing. I remembered Eileen's note. Her amah had said something about music. But if the house was empty? I shivered in the heat. Could ghosts turn on lights? It must be ghosts if the wife was dead, but . . .

'The husband!' I shouted. 'It must be him. Turning on the lights. Is he alive?'

'I don't know. Mum only said that he didn't live there any more. Shall I ask her?'

'Yes,' I said. 'Ask her what happened to the husband.'

The house looked almost ordinary in the sunshine, and I had no patience with ghosts just then. Wasn't I all involved with a fire-breathing dragon who lived at the top of the mountain?

'Are you going swimming afterwards?' said Vinnie as we went into the hut after break.

'Can't today,' I said. 'I'm busy. We're going to Huat Lee's, and then I'm going to write my story for the competition.'

'You've got a whole week. Why do you have to do it today?'

'I just want to, that's all.'

I saw the old man again at Huat Lee's that afternoon. He wasn't playing chess this time, but sitting just inside his room. Behind him on a shelf a big old wooden wireless was playing something. Someone was singing, but I couldn't understand the words. They weren't in English. The wireless crackled a lot, but you could still hear the melody. It went up and down like waves and curled out into the hot air of the shop like a fresh breeze, fanning me, cooling me. The man didn't really seem to be listening to the music. There was a book on his lap, too, but he wasn't reading it, just staring straight ahead of him.

I checked to make sure that my mother was busy at the counter, and then I said, 'Hello, do you remember me?'

He looked at me for a long time and said nothing. Then he shook his head. 'No, young lady. I'm sorry. I can't remember seeing you before.'

'But you must remember,' I burst out. 'It wasn't so long ago. You were sitting just there, playing chess . . .'

'It's possible. It's possible. I play chess a great deal.'

'But you don't remember me.'

'Do not be upset, my dear. The truth is, I remember very little. I find it better to forget as much as I can.'

Dad had said the man was strange and eccentric. I tried to feel sorry for him, but still, against all reason, I was cross with him for having forgotten about me and was just about to say goodbye and go and find my mother, when he began to speak again. I listened because I was there, standing right in front of him, but although he looked at me when he spoke, although he seemed to be speaking to me, I felt uncomfortable and a little frightened because I realized that he was looking at the place where I was without seeing me, and talking only to himself.

He said, 'Better to forget. Yes, undoubtedly. Better to be dead than alive, and better to be either than both dead and alive like me. A zombie. I call myself that sometimes, not one thing, nor the other. I remember too much. Songs, poems, places, things that made me happy once and now make me sad. Childhood. I wish I could forget everything but that. I try to think about it when I find myself dwelling on the sad things. In this hot country, I try to think of snow and riding through snow on a sleigh with bells. Making snowmen. Puddles in the spring. Blossoms on the trees. Dead leaves in the gutters. I miss the season. Always hot and wet, like living in an aquarium. My house when I was a boy was cramped and dark. A big black wooden corner cupboard with carved leaves on the door. And a piano. No, there was no piano. The rooms were too small. Why do I remember a piano? It's this Schubert. Only sounds, after all, but I wish I had not heard them again. I hate this music.'

'I think it's lovely,' I said, surprised. 'I wish I could understand the words.'

'Ah, the words. Love, springtime, flowers, a young man, a young woman beside a watermill. She is the miller's daughter. *Die schöne Müllerin*. That means "The Pretty Miller's Daughter." So beautiful, the music, so beautiful. It sings itself.'

Doesn't he hate it after all, I wondered. He went on as if he had read my thoughts.

'I hate it because it is so lovely, don't you see? And because I used to sing it when I was happy. You don't believe it, eh? That I had a voice once? Listen.' He joined in with the song, and his voice was firm and sweet, like a young man's voice, but he stopped after a short while and blew his nose in a large handkerchief, and did he wipe his eyes also, or did I imagine it?

'I must stop.' He coughed. 'This music makes me remember, and I try so hard not to remember. Pieces return anyway, floating back into my mind, and then I become unhappy again. The only safe time is today. I must think only about today. Today I will go to the dock and see the boat leave. That will be enough. Enough for one day.'

I couldn't think of anything to say. I muttered, 'Goodbye. I have to go and find my mother.'

'Do not tell her you have been talking to a crazy old man, to a zombie. She will be alarmed for you.'

'But I'm not frightened of you. And I don't really know what a zombie is.'

'Thank you,' he said. 'Thank you for not being afraid. Zombies are the walking dead. Dead people, walking around the earth in perpetual torment, as if they were alive.'

'You're not dead!' I cried, trembling. 'I'm talking to you.' I put out a finger and touched his hand. The skin felt dry and papery. 'I can touch you. You're alive.'

He smiled. 'It is most kind of you to say so. And I think it is true. On my good days, I must confess, I am glad that it is so.'

'I really must go,' I said.

'Yes, go. And if I forget you the next time, please remind me that you are the child who told me I was alive.'

All the way home in the car, I thought about the old man and what he had said. I had never heard of zombies before. While he was there in front of me, it was easy to see that he was alive, a real, living, breathing old man. But in the car I began to wonder. Why would he say he was a zombie if he wasn't? If there were dead people walking around pretending to be alive, they'd have to look real, wouldn't they, or everyone would guess their terrible secret. If the old man was one, then many other people could be: the gap-toothed woman who sat in the market, rocking backwards and forwards and smoking a pipe; the beggars I had seen in Singapore; the sailor on the boat that brought us here, whose face was white and pasty even though he worked long hours in the sun. Anybody could be a zombie, and you'd never know it. How could you ever tell?

'You're very quiet,' said Mum. 'Is anything wrong?'

'I'm thinking about the story I'm going to write for the competition,' I lied. 'I'm going to write a marvellous story. I'm going to try my hardest to win.'

'That's the stuff,' said Mum. 'Do your best. Doesn't matter if you win or not.'

It mattered very much, but I didn't say anything. Grown-ups had some funny ideas.

School Speech Day was in October, over a month ago now. I won the English prize and the History prize. The leather-bound books, covers stamped with the school crest in gold, were handed to me by a lady who resembled a dahlia: her hat was made of overlapping petals of shiny taffeta in a thousand shades of pink, and her thin, stalk-like body was encased in green jersey. Also, she nodded at people and swayed while she shook hands and moved as if blown by a gentle breeze. Walking back from the platform, I looked at all the pairs of pink hands clapping, and somehow couldn't believe it was for me.

All my life, as far back as I can remember, it seems that I've been writing. At school, you do it so much, you forget that it's going on, particularly during exams. Three hours to go, four questions to answer, pens out, cover the lines, race to catch up with your thoughts, get it down (and keep it legible), everything you've learned, quick, quick, before the time runs out. There. Finished. Phew. It never used to be like that. It used to be a pleasure. Of a sort. Not unmixed, because always, however much time there is, you know, you knew even when you were a child that there is a distance between the thoughts in your head and the words on the page that is impossible to bridge. All the fantastic imaginings of your brain, all those thoughts full of darkness and beauty and strange, unearthly things, lost something, lose something, as the hand fashions them into mere words, ties them down on to a page, makes them concrete. I knew all this when I was ten, though I never said it to myself in that way.

Thinking about it now, I realize what it was that made me enjoy writing so much in those days. I felt powerful. I could make things happen. I could invent places and people, I could make them as wicked and nasty and frightening as I liked without danger to myself. I could create heroes and heroines more beautiful and brave than anyone had ever dreamed of. I could control the climate, the geography, people's actions: everything. It was all mine, and no one else's. Later, much later, you say 'People don't act like this – this isn't true to life. This doesn't sound right,' and then the pleasure is diluted, but while it lasts, and whenever it returns, as it does from time to time, how you feel is omniscient and omnipotent, like a god.

7

As soon as Dad came home from work, I asked him for some of his office paper. It had blue lines and a wide pink margin, and it was so grand and grown-up look-ing that it nearly scared the story right out of my head. I sat at the table in the dining-room and wrote in an old exercise book. The beautiful paper lay on the table next to me, smelling the special smell of beauti-ful paper, and waiting for me to copy down my story on to it in my very best writing.

Once upon a time there was an Emperor who lived in China . . . the room I was in faded away as I began to write, and I was gone, into a world where em-broidered hangings fluttered on the walls, where narrow rivers flowed under bamboo bridges and past willow trees and plum trees in full bloom. There were the ladies of the court – I could see them dressed in robes of apricot and orange silk, their hair tied in shiny, lacquered knots on top of their heads, tiptoeing round the palace on tiny feet. The Emperor is there, with long fingernails and a long, black moustache.

His robe is purple, encrusted with gold threads, and slaves fan him with enormous fans painted with pictures of peonies and long-legged sea-birds. A visitor comes to the palace and tells the Emperor of a fabulous jewel, all the colours of the rainbow and shining with the light of a thousand stars. The jewel is hidden on the summit of a mountain on a faraway island, and is guarded day and night by a dragon so terrible and so monstrous that all who come to try to take the jewel are devoured and never heard of again. Their bones are strewn on the rocks around the cave, and jungle grasses grow out of their bleached skulls.

The Emperor is a greedy man, and like all Emperors, he has three sons. He promises his kingdom to the son who brings him back the wonderful jewel. They set sail for the island the very next day in their junks. The sails of the junks are like giant fans, and the ladies of the court stand at the water's edge and hide their tears behind small fans that move across their faces like butterflies, for who knows if any of the princes will ever be seen again?

'You must come and have supper now,' someone said. I looked, and after a moment, I recognized my mother. The motion of the boat on the rolling sea vanished, and there was my house all around me. I felt as though I had come back from a distant place and a long-ago time too quickly. All through supper, I thought about the princes, sailing towards the dragon's island. There would be a storm. I could imagine it clearly.

'Why aren't you eating, Flora?' asked Dad.

'I'm not very hungry. May I be excused?'

'It's nearly your bedtime, you know.'

'Yes,' I said. 'I know. Just let me do a little bit more. Just the storm and then I'll stop, I promise.'

The storm was marvellous. My waves towered like green glass walls, and crashed down on to the decks of the junks. The lightning split the sky into fragments, and the thunder sounded like the roar of the dragon himself. The wind plucked sailors from their posts and flung them like puppets against the sails. Some were washed overboard and never seen again, their screams lost, unheard in the hissing of the waters. But the princes survived, and the storm passed, and the next day they saw the island rising like a jewel out of water flecked with sunlight. An easterly wind blew the fragrance of flowers out to sea. The junks were pulled up on to the beach in a quiet spot, and the sons of the Emperor began the journey that was to take them to the foot of the mountain.

I couldn't fall asleep. The story went round and round in my head. Perhaps they could hear an ominous rumbling from the dragon's lair while they were still on the beach. Or maybe see flames on the mountaintop at night when they made camp and settled down to sleep. Then they would find the dragon, and see the jewel. I was looking forward to describing the dragon. They would fight him with swords, bombard him with huge metal balls heated in the fire until they glowed red, throw him poisoned meat, and in the end the youngest prince would snatch the jewel and everyone would run for the ships. There'd be an exciting chase over rocks and through jungles, and finally the princes would flee, all together in one junk. The dragon would swallow another boat whole, complete with its crew, and sink to the bottom of the sea. I hadn't decided about the jewel yet. Maybe it would fall into the sea as the princes scrambled aboard their boat, or maybe they would take it back to China and live happily ever after. I'd see tomorrow.

I should think about something else. Vinnie, telling me that the house was empty. Perhaps I'd imagined the whole thing. I untucked the mosquito net and jumped out of bed. The side of the mountain was black, darker than the dark sky. Then a light went on. I saw it. I watched it for a moment, and it moved, and grew dimmer, and then reappeared, as if someone were holding a lamp and walking from room to room. I shivered. I didn't care what Vinnie said, there was someone using the house at night. Who was it? As I crept back into bed, I thought of zombies.

Two days later, I gave my story to Mrs Aston.

'That was quick, dear,' she said. 'But it looks nice and neat. I hope you were careful about your spelling and punctuation.'

'Yes,' I answered, disappointed. Wasn't she going to ask about the story, about what happened? Should I tell her anyway? I opened my mouth to say something, but she pushed my carefully written pages into a pile of books in her bag and turned to the blackboard to write up the day's sums.

'I finished my story,' I told Vinnie.

'Already? Will you tell it to me? Is there time before the first lesson?'

'Yes,' I said. 'Listen.' I told her, and spoken out loud in the open air, the story sounded thin and not exciting at all, and I wondered how I could have been so thrilled by it as I wrote. Perhaps it wasn't as good as I thought?

'That's a good story,' said Vinnie. 'I bet it'll win.'

'No, it won't. It's feeble,' I said.

'I liked it,' said Vinnie.

I thought of my story all the time for the next few days. Sometimes I imagined the editor of the *Sabah Times* reading it, exclaiming over it, sweeping all the other entries to one side and crying: 'This is amazing! A clear winner! What powers of expression!' At other times, especially at night, I thought: it's not as good as I think it is. It's boring. Maybe he won't read past the first paragraph before throwing it aside, throwing it away. I had a clear daydream of my lovely sheets of paper, all the lovingly written words, torn into confetti-sized pieces, drifting in their thousands down into the editor's waste-paper basket, never to be seen again. Better to forget about the prize and about having my name in the paper. I ran to the back of the house, carrying the rough copy of my story. Kuta was burning rubbish in an old dustbin, and I tore the story into strips and threw the strips into the fire where they curled up in scarlet and black and shrivelled and vanished. Kuta said nothing, just pointed and smiled.

'It's rubbish,' I explained. 'I'm burning some old rubbish I found.'

Kuta nodded and poked the fire with a stick. It burned more brightly, and then subsided, and I looked at the grey, curly ashes that used to be my story and decided not to think about it any more. Or not quite so much, anyway.

'Come and play on Sunday morning,' said Vinnie before school on Friday.

'I can't. We're going on a launch picnic with the Winters and the Dicksons.'

'To Gaya Island?' asked Vinnie.

'I think so, yes.'

'Well, come after you get back. If there's time.'

'I wish you were coming,' I said.

'I wish I was, too. Launch picnics are lovely. You'll have to tell me all about it.'

'Oh, I will,' I said.

'And bring me a shell,' said Vinnie. 'You can find really big ones there.'

'Okay,' I said. 'I'll look for a really nice one to bring. D'you like the spiky ones with pink insides?'

'Anything big. I like big ones,' said Vinnie.

As I was coming back from the lavatory at break, I heard my name spoken. Chris and Eileen were sitting on the verandah of the hut with their backs to me, so I flattened myself against the wall and listened. Then I wished I hadn't.

Chris said: 'And Flora. That'll probably spoil everything. I wish you were coming instead.'

Eileen said: 'I do, too. But you won't have to play with Flora.'

'Oh, yes, I will.' Chris sounded fed up. 'Mother says I have to look after her, she's such a thin little thing, so delicate-looking. And play with her on the picnic because she's a girl and I'm a girl. She won't want to climb rocks or go diving or play shipwreck or anything. I'll probably have to sit on the beach all day with a book or something.'

'Why did you ask her, then?' said Eileen.

'*I* didn't!' Chris was indignant. 'Only, my mother knows her mother, and she invited them. I don't think it's fair, having to play with people who are drips, just because their parents are friendly with your parents.'

'Don't you like her at all?' Eileen asked. I held my breath, waiting for the answer, but Mrs Aston came out on to the verandah and rang the bell.

A drip. I was a drip. I couldn't get the word out of my head. It floated about behind my eyes and made me want to cry. Drip, drip, drip, like water off a roof. Wet. Soppy – oh, how horrible. I knew I wasn't brave, I never said I was daring, or good at climbing, but to be a drip – I couldn't bear it. I vowed to myself that on the launch picnic I would do every single thing that

Chris suggested and without batting an eyelid: that would show her.

'I was wrong,' she'd tell Eileen on Monday. 'Flora's not a drip at all. She's really one of us. You should have seen the things she did . . .' I thought of what Chris had said: climbing rocks, diving, playing shipwreck, and the thought of having to do them filled me with horror, but anything, anything at all, was preferable to being a drip.

The person who thought up picnics in the first place has a lot to answer for. Eating anywhere but at a table is asking for trouble. School picnics always seem to take place on windy days – sometimes there are even flurries of rain. Many's the bush I've huddled behind, trying to get warm, wearing a raincoat more often than not. Teachers on these picnics run about trying to convince us and themselves that actually it's all enormous fun and aren't we enjoying ourselves and isn't that the sun, look, over there, really on the point of coming out as soon as this tiny shower is over? As for the food, it's never what it should be. Oh, for champagne and cold chicken, strawberries, salmon mousses, lovingly packed into wickerwork hampers by maids in white caps and eaten by ladies in Leghorn hats and Liberty print dresses on a waspless summer day (is there such a thing?) under the branches of a noble elm in full leaf.

The truth is: it's two rolls with margarine spread lumpily all over them, a tomato, a hard boiled egg, a packet of crisps and a triangle of cheese so deftly wrapped in foil that getting into it requires the skills of a safebreaker. Oh, and a Penguin biscuit with half the chocolate smeared on the paper when you unwrap it. This feast is eaten on either a windblown hillside, or a windblown pebbly beach or a windblown bit of lawn in the grounds of a stately home. And the wasps are there in force, whatever the weather.

That launch picnic with the Winters and the Dicksons was the first of many. I don't think I fully appreciated them at the time. Perhaps the first picnic coloured the rest for me. It's difficult to describe them without sounding like a holiday brochure. The water was completely translucent all the way to Gaya Island. We looked over the side of the launch, and many feet below us every grain of sand, every fish and shell and coral was as clear as if the water had been a thin sheet of glass. We always set out very early in the morning, before it was too hot, and came back at lunch time and ate a huge curry lunch. I think about those curries a lot after meals of fatty mutton and rice pudding. There were little side-dishes of things to put on the curry and rice – sambals, they were called. Fried onions, raw onions, shredded coconut, fried bananas, tomatoes, mangoes, grated peanuts, pineapple, lime pickle, chutney – I counted twenty different sambals once at Vinnie's house. The cooks made the curry while we were on the picnics. I can remember thinking about that even then and wondering whether it was quite fair.

8

I was the only one in a little cotton sun-hat, like a child in an old-fashioned story-book.

'Do I have to?' I whispered to my mother.

'Of course you have to,' she answered in a voice that carried to every corner of the motor launch, a voice that must have reached Chris's ears even over the chugging of the engine. Why do mothers never realize the things that should be kept quiet? 'Don't you remember, you had a touch of the sun just the other day?'

'But Chris and Bob and Steve and Tony . . .' I began.

'They're used to it. They've lived here all their lives. And I've got a hat on too, haven't I?'

I said nothing. Couldn't she tell the difference between wide-brimmed plaited straw, with a red ribbon round the crown, and the 'Christopher-Robin-went-down-with-Alice' horror that I was forced to wear? I sat on the bench at the back of the launch, feeling miserable. We were all in bathing-suits, but I had to wear a shirt over mine, in case my shoulders got sore.

'Why are you wearing a shirt?' asked Tony.

'So I won't get burned,' I muttered.

'But you won't ever get brown if you wear a shirt all the time.'

'I'll have to stay white then, won't I?' I hissed through my teeth, and felt quite pleased when he blushed and said nothing and just went away. Perhaps I should hiss more often and let my eyes flash at people? It might be as useful as biting, if I got really good at it.

We had set off very early. The sky was still pearly, the sun low, hidden behind the mountain. But it was hot and there was no wind at all, so that the surface of the water shone like satin tightly stretched, with not a ripple or a lump anywhere. Our wake, as we spluttered along, sliced the pale green water and curled it into foam for a while, and then it closed up again behind the boat, smooth as oil, as if we had never disturbed it.

'What are you looking at?' Steve came and looked over the side with me.

'I'm looking for a dragon. I think there could be one down there.' As soon as I said it, I wished I hadn't. What would he think of me? But he only said: 'I'll look, too,' and leaned dangerously over the side.

'Is it big, do you think, or small?' he wanted to know.

'Huge. It swallowed some junks and sank to the bottom of the sea.'

'Really? Where did you hear that? Is it true?'

I giggled. 'No, silly. I made it up. For the story competition.'

'Tell me about it.'

So I told Steve, and he listened with his mouth half-open, and when I finished, he said, 'Gosh, that's a really wizard story. Bet you win a prize.'

'Do you really like it?'

'Yes. Have you got any other stories?'

'No, not exciting ones. Just about cats and horses and things.'

'That's boring. You should write exciting stories. I'd like to hear those.' And he was gone, to talk to Bob and Tony. For a moment, my fears about all that I would have to do on this picnic, my disgust at the babyish hat and shirt, even being called a drip – all the bad feelings disappeared, and I was sure that my story was marvellous and would win. I could see my name in letters half an inch high and thickly black, I could visualize my words neatly lined up in columns for everyone to read, and suddenly, everything seemed beautiful. Far away, down on the sea bed, clearly visible through twenty feet of transparent water, a small school of orange and silver fish darted about in the pale-grey branches of a coral forest and fluttered in and out of the hollows of huge, brown-flecked shells.

The grown-ups were laughing as we dropped anchor, two or three yards from the beach.

'Bob, Tony, Steve,' shouted Mr Dickson, 'how about a spot of diving for pennies?'

Shrieks of joy. Chris said: 'Me, too. I'm going too. It's not very deep, though.'

'Deep enough for you kids,' said Mrs Winters.

I watched, fascinated, as coins were thrown overboard. I could see them quite clearly lying on the sand, shining in the sun that filtered through the water. Bob, Steve, Tony and Chris immediately jumped up on to the side of the launch and dived in, and soon they were treading water near the boat, their hair plastered over their wet brown faces, their hands full of pennies. I could see Chris smiling. I could see two more pennies that had been left behind, still lying on the sand, and I heard Chris's voice in my head, telling Eileen what a drip I was. My parents weren't looking. I took off my glasses, my hat, my shirt and my sandals and laid them neatly on the bench. Then I climbed up on to the railings, and without stopping to think, dived clumsily overboard.

I hit the surface of the water and it stung my legs and stomach and the tops of my arms. My face felt as if someone had just slapped me hard. Why was it dark? Where was the sunlight? Why couldn't I see the pale sand? I realized that my eyes were closed. Was I supposed to open my eyes in the water? I had to, or I couldn't find the pennies. So I opened them, and immediately a fire seared my eyes. Fool, I thought, who ever heard of opening one's eyes in salt water? But I had to, or how could I see? I glimpsed something brown that I thought was a penny, just below me, and flailed about with my arms and legs, struggling to make my way down to the sand to pick it up, and I was nearly there, nearly, just a hand's length away, when I knew I had to breathe or else explode, and I pushed myself to the surface in one enormous lunge and gasped in mouthfuls of warm air. I was empty-handed. The pennies remained where they were, under the water.

Voices.

'Flora, darling, are you all right?' (My mother to me.)

'Silly girl, she's never dived before in her life.' (My mother to Mrs Winters.)

'Got to learn sometime.' (Mr Winters.)

'Why did you do it, Flora?' (My father.)

I said: 'There are still two pennies. Down there.'

Everyone laughed. Mr Dickson said, 'The things these children will do for extra money, eh?'

'I'll get them,' said Bob, who was near me in the water. He did a neat somersault, like a duck, and I could feel the water rushing past me as he swam about underneath my feet and came up a few seconds later with a penny in each hand.

'I think we'll give those to Flora,' said his father.

'But, Dad, I got them,' said Bob. 'It's not fair.'

'Flora tried. It was a jolly plucky try. Give them to her.'

Bob snorted and glared and gave them to me.

Later, on the beach, I said, 'Bob, you can have those pennies if you like. You got them up. I don't want them.'

'Neither do I,' said Bob. 'You keep them. You're just a little show-off.'

'I'm not!' I said. 'How was I showing off? Tell me!'

'I don't need to tell you. You were showing off to the grown-ups, and weren't they all impressed? Darling, delicate Flora, jumping overboard, fancy! It's nothing when we do it, it's ordinary for us, but when you do it, it's "Are you all right?" and "Isn't she brave?" You're nothing but a goody-goody.' He walked away. I went down to the edge of the water, scooped a hole in the wet sand and put the pennies in it. Then I covered them up. I didn't want them any more.

At about ten o'clock, we had cold drinks and sandwiches on the beach, then the grown-ups all pretended they were back on their own verandahs. Newspapers were taken out of bags, and so was knitting, and they just lay there on the sand as if it were a sofa and gossiped and laughed.

'Let's play Hide and Seek,' said Chris.

'Okay,' said Steve and Tony.

'Who's seeker?' said Bob.

'Last one over to that tree,' said Chris. 'We'll have a race. Everyone line up.'

We lined up on the sand and one of the grown-ups gave the signal, and off we all ran. And who came last? And who was going to spend the rest of the morning running around in the heat (with her hat on, Mum's orders) not finding the others? Flora the Drip, that's who.

'Now,' said Chris, 'you must count to a hundred and

then come after us. Anyone you find will help you find the others. Hiders have to try and get back to where the grown-ups are without being seen. Do you get it?'

'Yes,' I said. 'I think so.'

'Right,' she said. 'Turn around and cover up your eyes and start counting. Come on, you lot.'

I could hear their laughter growing fainter and fainter as I started to count.

Behind rocks, up trees, under creepers: I looked everywhere, for ages, and found no one. From time to time I ran and looked at the beach. No one had got to the grown-ups yet. Sweat was dripping into my eyes under the brim of my hat, and my feet were sore from so much walking. They'll never let me find them, I thought. They've gone right into the middle of the island, where the thick jungle is, and I'm not going after them there. I don't care. I bet it's full of snakes. I glanced up at a palm tree and saw a pair of feet.

'I see you, whoever you are,' I shouted. 'Come down.'

'Okay. It's me,' said Steve, and began to slip down the tree like a brown monkey. 'Anybody got to the beach yet?'

'I don't think so.'

'Well, I bet I know where some of the others are. Come on.'

I followed him, and we found Tony. Chris and Bob were waiting on the beach when we got back, laughing at something.

'Well,' said Chris, 'you found Steve, Flora. It's hard not to miss him, though. He's a rotten hider. Always up a tree, and his feet stick out. I bet Steve found Tony for you, didn't he?'

'Yes,' I said, and started walking away.

I walked for a while, and then I began to run. I thought of nothing. I felt sick. I wished I could have spent the morning with Vinnie. I would look for her shell. She'd be pleased. She liked me. What did it matter if no one else did?

'Hey! Flora, wait!' Steve was running after me. 'Stop a minute.'

'Why have you come after me? I'm looking for a big shell. What's the matter?'

'What's the matter with you? Why are you crying?'

'I'm not.'

'Yes, you are. I can see. Your face is all wet. Your mother said I should find you. We're nearly ready to go now. What's wrong? Haven't you had fun?'

I lost my temper. I turned on Steve and started shrieking at him: 'No, I have *not* had fun! Everyone's horrible. Nothing I do is right. No one ever says anything nice, and your sister's the worst of the lot. I hate her, and you, and all of them, and the water and the sun and the stupid picnic and I wish I'd never come.' I fell on to my knees and sobbed and sobbed.

Steve said, 'You mustn't mind Chris. She doesn't mean it, half the time.'

'But she's so brave,' I cried. 'She's so good at everything. She isn't scared of anything.'

'She's not good at everything,' Steve said placidly.

111

'You tell better stories. And she *is* scared of something, so there.'

'What?'

'I can't tell you. She'd kill me.'

'Please. I won't tell anyone. Please, Steve. Tell me one thing she's scared of.'

'She's scared of that house. You know the one. On the hill.'

'But why? You can't even see it from where you live.'

'She says there's a ghost up there. Because of what happened.'

I'd stopped crying by now. I said, 'What did happen there?'

'Nothing much.'

'Go on. Tell me. I promise not to tell.'

'Will you come back if I tell you? And cheer up?'

'Yes, I will. I promise. Please, Steve.'

'It's nothing much, honestly. A lady got drowned there. They had a pond in the garden, and this person just drowned.'

I thought of the fountain and the water lilies that Mrs James had spoken of.

'By accident, you mean?' I asked. 'Fell in and couldn't swim? It can't have been very deep.'

'Oh no,' Steve shook his head. 'She wanted to die. She was very unhappy.'

'Was it someone Chris knew?'

'It was Kristina, who was in the prison camp with my mother. You remember, the one who made the doll?'

'Yes,' I said. 'The one whose baby died.'

'That's the one. She used to live in that house. Now,

112

don't tell a soul what I told you. Chris is terrified of that house. She thinks it's haunted.'

So do I, I thought. I think it is, too.

I sat next to my mother on the journey back to Jesselton. Everyone was quiet: hot and tired, thinking of showers, and a large curry, followed by an afternoon nap. I looked at Chris. If only I could talk to her about the house, I thought, we could be scared together, but I can't. I promised Steve never to tell, and anyway Chris would never admit that she was frightened. Wouldn't she be amazed if I could show her, somehow, I don't know how, that the house and all its terrors didn't scare me a bit? She'd never get over it. I wish I could think of a way to do it. To show Chris, and the others, and myself. Am I really frightened of the ghost of a poor lady whose baby died? Didn't Mrs Winters say she was as beautiful as a princess, and kind? I'm not sure, anyway, if I believe in ghosts or not, and if I don't, then what is there to be frightened of?

As we landed, I remembered Vinnie's shell. I never found one for her, after all.

There was no light in the house that night. I looked at the black side of the mountain and thought about Kristina. She had made a beautiful garden. She had loved her baby. People used to go to tea at the house and have parties there. She had sung songs in the prison camp. She had made a doll for her child, and then given it to Chris. She was beautiful, and one day she died, with her long golden hair tangled up in the roots of the water lilies in her own pond. I shivered. Was it Kristina's ghost that visited the house in the darkness?

That night, I dreamed of empty rooms, empty and echoing. I dreamed of Kristina's baby, and the rag doll, and I could hear screaming, and see, somewhere at the very edge of my mind's eye, strands of long fair hair floating in muddy water, trailing like seaweed over white bones.

Wise people learn from experience, fools simply repeat their stupidities, which is, I suppose, why they remain fools. For example, I didn't know then, and I have not yet learned the very simple truth – call it Baxter's Law – that the more you look forward to something (an outing, or a party or any kind of treat) the less likely you are to enjoy it.

I remember the dance at the end of the summer term. It was to take place on the last Saturday. A local boy's school had been invited. We were going to be allowed to wear a little lipstick and powder and high-heeled shoes, and our evening dresses had been sent from home. Hanging next to my tunic in the narrow cupboard, the peacock blue taffeta seemed to be a magic garment, ready to transform my quite ordinary person into a figure of dazzling beauty. For nights before the dance, I had dreamed myself to sleep with the picture of a lovely me, waltzing in the arms of a slim, dark, young man, while all around I could hear whispers from my friends, from other young men, even from the staff: 'Isn't Flora looking beautiful? . . . That dress quite transforms her . . . I wish I could dance like that . . . will she have a dance free for me?' In these dreams, the supper table groaned under mountains of strawberries, cream in silver dishes, asparagus, slices of cold roast chicken: all the marvellous foods I could think of. The boys (young men) were all uniformly handsome, tall, polite and charming, and the one who danced with me was a sort of junior Fred Astaire.

The let-down began when I put on the dress. I stared at myself in Matron's full-length mirror. I looked all right, I suppose. The lipstick helped a little, and Kaye had put my hair up into a French plait.

'Very bonny,' said Matron, and she was probably right – a dreadful thought. I didn't want to look 'bonny,' a prettier version of myself. I wanted to become someone quite different, another person altogether, a dream person. The Hall was a disappointment, too. Of course, I had known all along that the dance was to be in the Hall; but somehow, the fantasy that took place in my head during the looking-forward period was set among marble columns and floors polished to the sheen of glass, and all the chairs had red velvet seats. I wasn't ready for the ordinariness of it. And the boys, oh dear, the boys! That was what they were, alas. Some were pleasant, some boring, some even quite handsome, but they were all young, like us – not suave, not sophisticated, and not a Fred Astaire among them. We had cocoa at eleven o'clock in Miss Travis's study. Cocoa, the acme of romance. My pretty satin slippers had black marks all over the front, where my partners had trodden on my toes.

Everything's like that: less than you thought it would be, not as wonderful as you imagined when it filled your dreams.

9

At breakfast the next day, my father passed me the newspaper and said, 'Here's something that will interest you.' I looked. The letters stretched and shrank and danced about so that I could hardly read them. After a while, they settled into a pattern. There it was on the left-hand side, in bigger print than all the other headlines: 'Flora Baxter wins first prize in Essay Competition.' On an inside page they had printed the story, just as I had written it. It took up two whole columns. At the top, my name was printed again:

The Legend of Kinabalu by Flora Baxter.

It looked strange. Even the name did not seem to belong to me, and the neat black newspaper letters altered the words I had written so that I hardly knew them for my own.

Dad read the story, and then Mum, and then Kuta and Shau Yee came in and were shown where my name was, and everybody smiled and kissed me and was pleased. Happiness crept over me like a blush, filling up every part of my body. I couldn't eat my breakfast. I couldn't really hear what anybody said to me. The words 'I've won, I've won, I've won' sang themselves over and over in my head.

Suddenly, I heard a shout of 'Flora!' from the compound, and Vinnie bounded up our verandah steps and almost fell into the dining-room.

'Have you see the paper, Flora? You've won!' Everyone laughed as she pulled me off my chair and, tugging my hand, dragged me outside, where we shrieked and screamed and jumped up and down and tore up handfuls of dry grass and threw them up into the air.

I had calmed down by school time. Mrs Aston told everyone about my triumph.

'I think Flora deserves a clap, children, don't you? Well done, Flora dear. We're all very proud of you.' Everyone clapped, and I blushed and said thank you, and that was that. Steve said: 'I told you it was a good story,' and no one else mentioned it. By the end of the morning, I realized that perhaps my achievement was not as startling as I had thought it was. Perhaps I had only won because all the other stories were absolutely dreadful? It seemed quite likely.

'There's going to be a tea-party at the Club on Saturday, isn't there?' said Vinnie at break. 'Everyone will come. You'll have to wear a party frock. Maybe you'll have to make a speech. You'll have to go and shake hands with the editor of the newspaper. Gosh, I'm longing for it.'

'I'm not,' I said. 'I shall feel a fool.'

'You're silly,' Vinnie declared. 'I wish it was me. I'm going to eat tons of sandwiches and drink gallons of iced lemonade. Do you think the Governor will be there? Maybe the Police Band will play on the Padang as his car arrives. Maybe they'll even play as your car arrives.'

I laughed. 'Rubbish! There'll probably be no one there at all, just you and me, and my mum and dad, and the editor, holding the pen and pencil set.'

I didn't really think so. I was just pretending. All through the history lesson, I imagined what the Club would look like, decked with flags in my honour, all the ladies in garden party dresses and frothy hats, and the Governor wearing his plumed white helmet and presenting me with a medal on a shiny blue ribbon, a kind of extra prize. The photographer would be there, and my picture would appear in the paper. Underneath, it would say: 'Smiling Flora Baxter, the young winner of the *Sabah Times* Essay Competition, receiving her prize.' I will wear my blue organza dress, I thought, as Mrs Aston's voice went on and on about King Harold at the battle of Hastings. I don't care if I will be hot. I shall ask Vinnie if Ah Yin will wash my hair in coconut oil and make it shine.

All the ladies will say to one another, 'How pretty she looks! What a darling! Isn't that a pretty dress?'

* * *

The morning went by very quickly. I never once thought about Kristina, or her ghost, or the house, or even what Chris was thinking of me. I was in a long and beautiful daydream until the bell was rung for the end of school.

'Hurry up with the lipstick, Flora. You're taking ages.' Vinnie had tied a red scarf round her head so that it hung down her back, like long, wavy red hair. I gave her the lipstick.

'You never answered me,' I said.

'What about?'

'About what I told you. You know, about Kristina and the baby and everything. Do you think the house is haunted?'

'I don't care if it is.' Vinnie's voice sounded funny when she stretched her mouth wide open to put the lipstick on. 'I don't believe in ghosts.'

'Why don't you?'

'Because I've never seen one.'

'That's stupid. You've never seen a volcano either.'

'But I know they're true. There's a picture in our geography book. You've never seen a photograph of a ghost.'

I thought about this. 'That's because they're kind of transparent. They wouldn't show up.'

Vinnie laughed. 'Even if there are such things, I've never understood why people are afraid of them. Why should a poor dead woman, who was jolly nice when she was alive, bother you? She can't hurt you.'

Vinnie had finished reddening her mouth and was

busy choosing earrings to go with her new red hair. I looked at her without seeing her, thinking about what she had said. She was right. If a ghost lurked in the empty house, it couldn't possibly hurt me. Why would it want to? An idea began to form in my mind.

'Vinnie?'

'Mmm?'

'I'm going up there.'

'Where?'

'To the house.'

'What, now?'

'No, silly. On Sunday . . . there's the tea-party at the Club on Saturday.'

'But why?' Vinnie put her earrings on the dressing table and turned to face me.

'Because I want to see what it's like. Because if I go there, really go there, then I'll know that what you're always telling me is true, that it's just a boring old empty house, and there are no ghosts there or anything.'

'Why don't you get your mum and dad to drive you up?'

'No, I want to do it on my own. To show . . . that I can.'

'I know why.' Vinnie grinned. 'You want to be able to tell Chris. You know she's scared of the house, and you want to do something she can't do, don't you?'

'But how did you know?' I whispered. 'Steve told me on the picnic. He said it was a deadly secret.'

'He tells everyone that. Everyone knows. Honestly.' (Horrible, horrible Steve, letting me think that I was special!)

'Then why don't they ever mention it?'

'Eileen did once,' Vinnie pirouetted in front of the mirror. 'Chris took scissors and cut up Eileen's skirt. We don't talk about it now.'

'I'm going up there,' I said. 'On Sunday. I'll tell Mum and Dad I'm coming to your house in the afternoon. May I borrow your bike?'

'Don't you want me to come, too? I wouldn't mind, honestly.'

Yes, I wanted her to come more than anything. Already, the thought of going up the hill to that place made me feel a little sick.

'No, thanks,' I said. 'I must go on my own. You can call the police and tell my parents if I don't come back.'

'Why ever shouldn't you come back? There's absolutely nothing up there but a house.'

I would go in bright sunlight, I thought. Ghosts don't haunt in the sunlight, surely? Dead of night, that was the time. There was nothing to be scared of, nothing at all. Then why was I scared?

'Are you ready?' said Vinnie.

'Yes,' I answered.

'Come on, then,' she said, and we went into the sitting-room and pretended to be film stars and danced around and sat with our legs crossed and used Dad's long yellow pencils to be cigarettes in cigarette holders.

On Saturday, we drove to the Club at tea time for the presentation of my prize. The blue organza dress was tight under the arms, and the fabric was scratchy on the backs of my legs as I walked. There was no Police Band, and everybody in the Club seemed to be drinking tea and talking as usual and looking at the magazines. Only a handful of people from school had arrived, and Mrs Aston was the only lady in a garden party frock. Everyone else was in normal clothes. A few sardine sandwiches and tomato sandwiches were set out on a table. The editor sat at another table with the prizes in front of him. He looked like any other man. He had a moustache. He wore khaki shorts. He didn't look like a powerful and mysterious being at all. I sat on a chair next to the prize winners from other schools. Our names were called, mine last of all, and we each came forward and took our prize and went to sit down again.

'Jolly good, Flora,' said the editor, as he shook my hand.

'Thank you,' I said. Everyone clapped. Vinnie shouted 'Hurray!' but her voice faded and disappeared very quickly. People had started talking again. We all ate the sandwiches and drank lukewarm lemonade. Mrs Aston sparkled and smiled and chatted to everyone as if she were at Government House, but there was no sign anywhere of the Governor and his hat with the white plumes on it.

But oh, the prize! The prize was really beautiful. Grey velvet in the box, like soft fur, and on the velvet, a grey pen and pencil, each with a gold top. The gold was dull and shiny in stripes, and the clips had tiny gold arrows at the end. Imagine the words that you could write with such a pen, think of the delicate lines the pencil would make as it traced the outline of an island or a continent on the white page. Who could ever make a mistake with such beauty in their hands? I stroked the velvet and turned and turned the pen under the light to see it shine and thought that surely there would be magic in everything I wrote from now on.

There's a funny thing that I've noticed about ghosts – everyone who believes in them and is ready to regale you with the most ghastly tales has always heard the story first from someone else: a cousin, a friend, a grandmother. No one ever says casually in conversation 'I saw an amusing ghost yesterday.' The same old stories turn up again and again – the faceless driver who picks up a hitchhiker on a dark and stormy night, the conversations people have with normal beings who later turn out to have been dead for years, and so on. The tellers of these stories seem to have driven themselves into a rut as far as the décor of the hauntings is concerned. Literature is partly to blame, I suppose. Ghosts, traditionally, are associated with darkness, cold, old dark houses, cemeteries, churchyards, chains, moans, groans and the rattle of ancient bones. Why not a haunted launderette? Or supermarket? Why not a spectre doomed to an eternity of handing out buns and cocoa in a school canteen? As far as character is concerned, all ghosts are tarred with the same brush: frightening, cruel, desperate spirits motivated by grief, despair and revenge, after someone's blood – or anyone's. This seems illogical. Why shouldn't departed spirits exhibit the same differences in temperament as living people? Why no fat, jolly ghosts, or boring, silly ghosts, or attractive, smiling ghosts in high-heeled red satin shoes? It seems unfair.

When I was ten years old and thinking of cycling up the hill to the Schneider house, I believed in every frightening thing it was possible to believe in. The things that terrify me now are real: bombs that can wipe out whole continents, diseases specially invented by scientists in laboratories – all the dreadful things that people can do, have done, are doing to each other, so that a restful ghost or two, dissolving through a wall here, or rattling the odd chain there, would come as quite a relief.

And yet, and yet . . . I left my blazer in one of the piano practice rooms yesterday. When I went back to fetch it, it was half-past four and there was only a smear of grey light left in the sky. I didn't bother to turn on any lights; I knew exactly where I wanted to go. I walked along the corridor and into Room Number Three and picked up my blazer. Someone had left the door of Number Two open, and the piano wasn't closed either. Some silly first year, I thought. I'll just go in and close the lid and shut the door and make everything tidy. But I couldn't. I looked at the piano standing there alone, open and empty; I looked at the gathering darkness outside the uncurtained window. The piano stool was slightly crooked, as if someone had pushed it back a little . . . I ran back into the lighted school corridor, holding my blazer so tightly clutched in my fingers that when I shook it out, it was creased all down the front. I laughed about it afterwards (the ghost of some poor child doomed to an eternity of chromatic scales), but the next time I go into the practice rooms, I shall turn on all the lights.

10

'What do I need a water bottle for?' I asked.

'You'll be glad of it later,' said Vinnie. 'You'll see. It's quite a long way up that hill.'

I said nothing. It felt like miles and miles even before I set out.

'It's three o'clock now,' said Vinnie, 'If you're not back by half-past five, I'll tell your parents, and they'll come and look for you.'

'They'll kill me if they ever find out,' I whispered.

'Why? It's not such a terrible thing. You're only going on a bike ride.'

'But I lied to them. I said I was going to be with you.'

'You *are* with me, silly. I'll say the bike ride idea only came to you when you got here. If I have to say anything. The things you find to feel nervous about, honestly. You'll be back ages before half-past five anyway. Don't worry. You'll just have a quick look and come back, won't you?'

'Yes,' I said.

'Come and get the bike out then.'

I followed Vinnie to the garage.

*   *   *

I rode past Kampong Aya and took the road that forked to the right, up the mountain. A few old men squatting on the grass nodded as I rode by, but the women were all at the market. Perhaps I would see them coming home when I rode back. If I rode back. Of course I would ride back. What would Vinnie say if she knew I was thinking like this? I avoided looking at the house and stared at the road in front of me. The slope of the hill was becoming quite steep, and the sun hammered down on my forehead. I wished I'd brought my stupid hat after all. I don't know why I didn't. What did it matter what you wore to a haunted house? Suddenly, putting on clean shorts and a shirt seemed silly, but when I'd dressed in the morning, I'd had a vague idea that I should look as neat as possible, perhaps because of the parties that used to be held in the house.

I'd told Vinnie when she remarked how tidy I was and she'd answered: 'You don't even want a ghost to think badly of you, do you?' and laughed.

'There are no ghosts,' I'd said.

'But you're expecting to meet someone, dressed like that.'

'It's just in case I do.'

'That white shirt will be all sticky and sweaty by the time you're half-way up that hill.'

She was right.

The road stopped a short way from the house, and then there was only a reddish, dusty track to cycle on.

It was so steep that I got off and walked, pushing the bicycle. Looking back, all I could see was a bushy green mass of creepers and trees between me and the road, which wound like a small grey snake a long way below me. I felt shut in, as if the vegetation had grown thicker behind me, covering the path back so that I could never get out, so that no one could ever drive in and find me, and I would spend forever locked on this hill with whatever faceless terror the house contained.

There was an old van parked crookedly under some shrubs beside the path. It looked dusty, neglected, as if no one had driven it for years. Perhaps it had belonged to the owner of the house, and he had left it there a long time ago. I looked through the open window. There was a newspaper on the seat. That'll tell me how long the van has been here, I thought, and put my hand in and picked up the paper. I looked at the date. 'Saturday May 9, 1953,' it said. Yesterday. Someone had been in this car as recently as that. Maybe they were still here.

'Is anybody there?' I shouted, but there was no answer. Perhaps the owner of the van was hiding somewhere, waiting to pounce on me.

'You'd better not come near me,' I yelled. 'The police know I'm here. I told them. Inspector Ian Aston himself is on his way.' I thought of Mr Aston in his neatly pressed khaki shorts and felt a little better. I walked on until the dusty track ended, and I realized that I was in the garden, and there straight ahead of me was the house.

Vinnie had been right. I was hot and sweaty and thirsty. I sat down on a tree stump and looked around as I took a few gulps from my water bottle. A field of very long, dry grass stretched between me and the house. There was a path laid with flag stones leading up to the steps, but the mosses and weeds had almost buried it.

Once, when I was frightened in the night, Kuta had come into my room and told me of a child who was scared of a dragon's head that passed by the house in the darkness, and the child's mother had led him right up to the dragon, and when the child touched the hideous face, his fear vanished, for he saw that it was only a mask made from layers of painted paper. 'Look at what frightens you, Flora,' Kuta had said. 'Look in its eyes, and the fear will be gone.' I looked at the house and looked away, and then looked back again. It did seem less frightening. There was a verandah with pretty columns, which had once been painted white, holding up the roof. The second floor made the house seem very large, after the long, low bungalows beside the sea. All the shutters were closed. Some had creepers growing over them, It looked as if the house had closed its eyes against the sun. Dusty, peeling and sad . . . and totally empty. I took another sip from my bottle. Kuta was right, but still, would I have the courage to open the door and walk into the empty rooms? I decided to explore the garden first.

I walked along the stone path and round the side of

the house. The ground sloped away to the left, and at the bottom of a little hill, there was a hedge, all green branches crossed and tangled and spiked with enormous thorns, like a picture from 'Sleeping Beauty,' of the briar hedge that grew round the castle when everyone had fallen asleep for a hundred years. I walked all around the thicket, and on the other side there was an opening, as if the Prince had been there before me and hacked a path through with his magic sword. I could see the small pond, right in the middle of the circle of bushes. It was a large stone basin, dry now, with a statue of a fish at the centre. This is the pond, I thought, this is where is happened. If there's a ghost to see, this is where I shall see it. I looked all around. Nothing. I walked right up to the edge of the pond and wrote my name in the reddish dust that lay over the stone and I was not frightened. I laughed as I realized that my fear had vanished and began to imagine how the roses would have looked long ago, when Kristina was alive to look after them, before their branches had become locked and tangled into one another.

I found a rosebud. One small rosebud, green, with pale yellow petals just showing at the tip, and I picked it and threw it into the basin for Kristina and her baby. I felt I should do something, say a prayer or sing a hymn, to make the occasion more dignified, almost like a funeral, and I was just wondering what would be most suitable, when I heard piano music and the sound of a man singing. I stood as still as the fish in the centre of the fountain, cold as ice suddenly, and

131

every fear I had ever had in the world seemed locked up with me in that circle of thorns. There was nowhere else it could be coming from. Someone was inside the house. I sat on the edge of the pond, wondering if I could creep round the house and back to my bicycle before the song was finished. The only thought in my head was how to get home, out, down the hill as quickly as possible. Chris, and telling Chris that I had been to the house, all of a sudden seemed very unimportant, and I shut my eyes and said, in a whisper, 'O God, please let me get safely back and not see any ghosts and I'll be good for ever and ever and I won't mind about anything Chris says to me. Please, please let me have the courage to get to my bike.' I kept my eyes closed, half expecting to be magically wafted down the hill in a pillar of smoke, but nothing happened, and soon the music began to soothe me, like a lullaby. Somewhere (where?) I had heard it before, music like water, cooling music, and I couldn't think where. Perhaps Mrs James had played it? I didn't think so, but I'd heard it, and the tiny part of me that wasn't busy being terrified, listened and grew bigger and bigger until I noticed that I was no longer afraid. I felt as if I were in my own dream, as if I could pinch myself at any moment and wake up under the mosquito net at home. I stood up and opened my eyes and walked out of the overgrown rose garden, up the hill towards the house.

I followed the music. I stood on the verandah and listened, and then I pushed the door open and walked in. The sunlight made yellow stripes on the dusty floor. The room was empty, except for a small table by the window with an oil lamp on it. The glass shade of the lamp was patterned with leaves, and there was a photograph next to the lamp of a woman in a bride's dress, with a lace train foaming round her feet like a wave. I walked through the room and stood by an open doorway leading to another room. There was the piano, and sitting at the keyboard was the old man from Huat Lee's back room: the chess player, the zombie. I tried as hard as I could to feel frightened, but the music and the singing, his voice, singing so beautifully, made all my fear dissolve, and I stood there for a long time, watching his white hair blowing in the draught made by the big fan on the ceiling.

I clapped when he finished playing. 'Lovely,' I said. 'That's lovely.'

'Yes,' he answered. He didn't seem surprised to see me. 'It's Schubert.'

'What does it mean, what you've been singing? What do the words say?'

'The words? Oh, a young man is asking a brook if his love loves him or not. He asks a brook because he cannot ask a star or a flower. It is . . . not very sensible.'

'I heard it . . . that day in Huat Lee's, do you remember?'

'Ah, yes, you are that child. Of course, of course. Today is a good day for remembering.'

'Do you come here a lot?' I asked.

'Certainly I come. This is my home.'

'Your home? But there's no furniture, and the house is empty . . .' My voice faded away.

'I did not say I lived here. I said it is my home. I sleep and eat and read somewhere else, but here I live, I am alive.'

'I'd be scared . . . to come to such a lonely place. Aren't you frightened? Some people say it's haunted.'

'Haunted? Yes, of course it is.'

'Is it?' Here was a grown man telling me . . . but Dad had said he was eccentric . . . a new fear prickled my spine. I was alone in an empty house with a madman. I said quickly, 'Have you seen a ghost?'

'It's not as easy as you think.' He sighed. 'I feel them here. I come because I can feel them, and I sing to them because I know she loved the music.' He paused. 'Oh, yes, we had evenings here, full of music, full of singing, and Lily James would dance. Everybody came. We had lanterns on the verandah. The ladies wore silk dresses. I think, sometimes, that they can still hear me, and that the music is like a message saying that I have not forgotten them, and that I still love them.'

'But . . . who *are* they?' I asked. I asked even though I knew, even though I had known the moment I saw him at the piano. Why had I never asked Dad to tell me his name?

'My wife Kristina,' he said 'and my baby, Liesel. Kristina died down there, in the pond, in the water. Liesel in a prison camp.'

I said 'My friend . . . she's called Christine, too. She has the doll that . . . your wife made for Liesel. I've seen it.'

134

For a long time the man said nothing, then: 'I know. I used to see the Winters a great deal. After Kristina died, they came for a while, but then they stopped. I think they were embarrassed. The British are embarrassed by too much of anything – grief, love, laughter, fear. Forgive me' – he bowed – 'I know you are British, of course, and I do not wish to be impolite.'

'It's quite all right,' I said. 'May I ask you something?'

'With pleasure.'

'Do you come here at night sometimes? I've seen a light, from my bedroom window.'

'Yes, I come and sit in the lamplight sometimes. When I feel especially lonely, then I think of poor Kristina all alone out there in the dark, and I turn on the lamp. I have thought . . . during the past decade it has been easy to think, has it not? . . . that there is too much darkness in the world.'

I did not understand what he was saying. Perhaps he was being mad again?

'They are all dead,' he said. 'Millions are dead. All my family. The ones left behind in Germany, too. Too much darkness.'

I thought of Vinnie and looked at my watch.

'I have to go now,' I said.

'Please come again.' He smiled at me.

'Yes, thank you. Will you play more music?'

'I shall always play. Until I die. And when I die there will be no one here to play for me, and the jungle will cover the house, and it will be as though we had never existed.'

'I'll remember you,' I said.

His eyes lit up. 'Yes, yes, perhaps you will. I shall try to think that you will. But the memory will be like this house – other memories will grow over it, cover it up, hide it, until, when you are as old as I am, you will have to dig deeply to find it.'

'I must go now,' I said, edging towards the door. 'Goodbye.'

'Goodbye. Remember me to Christine Winters. Tell her . . . tell her Santa Claus sends his love.'

'Santa Claus?'

'She will know.' He chuckled. 'We gave a party, at Christmas. Christine was two, maybe even less. And I found a costume, and I thought – we thought – that it would amuse the child and remind us of home. It's very hard, making a proper Christmas here, in the heat. Christine was very frightened. She cried and cried and had to be taken out, taken home. I'm sure her mother will have reminded her of it, over and over, at every Christmas.'

'I'll tell her,' I said. 'Goodbye.'

He had gone back to the piano. I heard the music growing fainter and fainter as I ran across the long grass to my bicycle.

'And then?' Vinnie asked.

'Nothing. I rode home. Here I am. I did it, I did it, I did it; I went there and saw everything and spoke to Mr Schneider, and I'll tell Chris and she'll never believe me, and then I'll remind her about Santa Claus, and she'll *know* it's true.' I hugged Vinnie. 'And

136

there are no ghosts, no ghosts, no monsters, no zombies, nothing, only a poor, sad old man. Oh, I'm so happy. I could dance. I shall dance all the way home. 'Bye, Vinnie. Thanks so much for the bike and the water bottle and everything.'

' 'S okay. 'Bye, Flora. See you tomorrow.'

Of course, the light was on in the house that night, but now it seemed like a kiss blown into the darkness. Perhaps Mrs James had been thinking of Kristina when I had seen her, that first night, on her darkened verandah?

'Chris?'

'Yes?'

'Can I tell you something?' We were sitting under the frangipani tree, waiting for Mrs Aston to arrive and open the school hut.

'Okay.'

'I went up there yesterday. To the Schneider house.'

'Don't believe you. You wouldn't dare.' Chris broke off a piece of grass and began to chew it.

'I did. I borrowed Vinnie's bike. I saw the pond and everything, and there are no ghosts, only poor Mr Schneider who goes there and plays the piano sometimes.'

'He's batty. He won't see anyone or speak to any of his old friends. I don't think you saw him at all.'

'I did, and he remembers you. You cried when he dressed up as Santa Claus when you were little. He said to send you love from Santa Claus.'

Chris stood up. 'I never did believe all the stories about ghosts. I guessed it was him, really.' She kicked a stone. 'Mrs Aston's car's coming. D'you want to come and watch her kissing Mr Aston goodbye?'

'Okay,' I said, and followed her down to the road.

That's the story. I think when Chris asked me to come and watch Mrs Aston with her I thought everything would be different. I thought that she would be my friend and admire me as I admired her. I also thought that what I considered to be my first brave action would lead inevitably to others. But I still couldn't jump on to the garage roof or run fast or climb trees or play a proper game of Cowboys and Indians. Chris still thought I was a drip, and nothing was very different from what it had been before. Perhaps I learned, if I learned anything, that there I was, me, as I was, and that I could fiddle with this and tinker with that, but that deep down nothing could really be altered and that in the end it was impossible to be someone else. Oh, you try. You dance, and you act, and you change your clothes and your hair and your make-up, and you write yourself into stories in a thousand disguises, but when all that's over, there's your old self at the centre. Hello, hello! Fancy meeting you here when all the time I thought it was Mata Hari, Odette,

Florence Nightingale, Charlotte Brontë, Judy Garland, Sarah Bernhardt . . . only Flora Baxter after all.

And Mr Schneider? He died a long time ago of pneumonia, which is a silly disease to die of in the tropics. Rain had soaked him one night as he walked across the garden to the house, but he played the piano nevertheless and the lighted lamp stood in the window to light up the night, for his wife, his child and the millions who had died before them. Kristina and Liesel meant something to me. Even though I had never seen them, they were names, they were faces, I could imagine them. But millions – millions is like stars or grains of sand. Who has the imagination to conceive of the death of millions? Thinking of it can drive a person mad.

Mr Schneider thought of it and was haunted by all the deaths, haunted by memories, and he served them until he died.

I can remember how happy I was, how relieved to discover that there were no ghosts after all. I felt lighter without the weight of that fear upon me. And now, having written this, *because* I have written it, I find that I was wrong all along. Mr Schneider had his ghosts, and he has become mine.